RINGO,
THE ROBBER
RACCOON

Also by Robert Franklin Leslie

The Bears and I
High Trails West
In the Shadow of a Rainbow
Miracle at Square Top Mountain
Read the Wild Water
Wild Burro Rescue
Wild Courage
Wild Pets

RINGO, THE ROBBER RACCOON The True

Story of a Northwoods Rogue

ROBERT FRANKLIN LESLIE
Illustrated by Leigh Grant

DODD, MEAD & COMPANY NEW YORK

Text copyright © 1984 by Robert Franklin Leslie
Illustrations copyright © 1984 by Leigh Grant
Distributed in Canada by
McClelland and Stewart Limited, Toronto
Manufactured in the United States of America

1   2   3   4   5   6   7   8   9   10

Library of Congress Cataloging in Publication Data

Leslie, Robert Franklin.
    Ringo, the robber raccoon.

    Summary: An account of the close friendship the author
developed with a solitary wild raccoon while searching
for signs of the Sasquatch in the British Columbia
wilderness around Lake Nicomen.
    1. Raccoons—Biography—Juvenile literature.
2. Black bear—Biography—Juvenile literature.
[1. Raccoons.   2. Forest animals.   3. Sasquatch.
4. Natural history—British Columbia]   I. Grant,
Leigh, ill.   II. Title.
QL795.R15L47   1984   599.74′443   83-25505
ISBN 0-396-08323-4

Dedicated to

Florine Holder

with deepest affection

Much that I sought I could not find;
Much that I found I could not bind;
Much that I bound I could not free;
Much that I freed returned to me.

LEE WILSON DODD
Ronde Macabre

Contents

Author's Note

THIS true adventure took place recently in southern British Columbia. Geographic locations mentioned are the actual places where all events came about.

Filled with details of this exploit, my notebook recalls mostly the behavior of a raccoon whom I called Ringo. Without comparing his motives and scandalous conduct with human urges and behavior, I have reported exactly what he did on each occasion—as a typical raccoon—and what happened as the result of his saucy impulses to rob his neighbors. My notes also reflect many native Indian beliefs about wild animal behavior, especially that of bears and raccoons.

Although I never forgot that Ringo was a *wild* animal, it was often difficult to exclude my own sentimental notions concerning raccoons. Because of deceitful facial expressions, guiltless body poses, and "hands" with babylike fingers, Ringo's very acts of sneak-thievery seemed at first out of character. Raccoon cunning and violence came to me as a startler in light of so much reading about natural behavior and innocence among wild creatures. Imagine my shock upon discovering that wildlings plan every shade of willful deceit, muggings, theft, burglary—even murder—all against their own kind as well as other species.

The fact that Ringo was habitually naughty didn't render him hopelessly unattractive. On the contrary, he practiced many delightful actions that brainwashed me into loving him and possibly acting as an artificial influence. Because of my fondness for this rascal, I collaborated in battles he never would have started had I not been there to reinforce his outrageous offenses.

In addition to strong-arm tactics, he was a "gentleman" thief. As such, his snooty conduct presented an exciting question: What could explain his friendly and honest association with certain species and sneaky robbery of others? In order to take advantage of my life-style and at the same time perfect his "art" of thievery, he gave up most nighttime habits of his kind: hunting, feeding, associating with other raccoons.

And speaking of food, he often pretended to be a gourmet, which he was *not*. Yet occasionally he disregarded many natural food items that most raccoons eat with gusto so that he could swindle tastier morsels from my plate—another facet, no doubt of my unnatural influence. In this same light, I blame myself for the precious autumn time he squandered in my company when he should have been fattening himself for hibernation.

From the beginning of our friendship one fact stood out like the black mask on Ringo's face: His rollicking behavior made me suspect him of a *plan* or driving *motivation*, his big secret in the back of that brilliant head.

ROBERT FRANKLIN LESLIE

1

A Thief in Camp

LOW-HANGING clouds, swishing rain, and belchy thunder gave the night of July 1 a mysterious and scary mood. Hissing louder than any normal gale, a southwesterly chinook flogged the forest behind my campsite. Midnight whirlwinds spouted across the sprawling basin of British Columbia's Nicomen Lake, churning up frothheads that shuffled like ghosts on the water. The restless lake seethed under every flash of lightning. Lodgepole pines, larch, and spruce swayed and creaked above my pup tent, threatening every moment to crash to earth and squash me in my sleeping bag. It was the kind of night you'd expect a ghost to snoop through camp.

Shortly after midnight an avalanche of cooking utensils clattered even louder than the storm. To me the ruckus suggested that Sasquatch, the most terrifying creature in the Northland, might be in the act of raiding my knapsack! Before retiring, I had thrown a tough nylon rope over a high limb to suspend my food and utensils in order to prevent black bears and pack rats from freeloading.

Impossible that any animal short of Sasquatch, the legendary Bigfoot ape-man, could reach the canvas rucksack. He was supposed to be taller than a basketball player. Too panic-stricken to use the flashlight, I slipped farther into the sleeping bag, covered my head, and remained motionless. While looting my pack, the horrible beast mumbled in a high-pitched voice.

Hoping to locate and study Bigfoot colonies, a society of conservationists in California had hired me to explore the wilderness around Manning Provincial Park in southern British Columbia, an area reputedly rich in Sasquatch clues. The purpose of my one-man expedition was to find footprints, make plaster of Paris castings, and send them to Los Angeles for scientific study. The society had ordered me to sneak a few snapshots of the beast himself—if, of course, I didn't chicken out. A photographer named Roger Patterson, traveling through Northern California's Bluff Creek wilderness in October, 1967, crowded the Viet Nam War out of newspaper headlines with his twelve-second movie of a Sasquatch escaping into a forest. Soon after Mr. Patterson's film had been shown by every agency of the press and TV, many outdoorsmen in the Pacific Northwest came forth to report sightings of the "American Yeti" . . . Sasquatch . . . Bigfoot. Certain Indians in British Columbia also included the ape-man in their campfire tales. Hunters still tell of eight-foot-tall "gorillas" they have seen in the Canadian Cascade Mountains near the United States border—Manning Park, to be specific . . . Nicomen Lake. The monster had "definitely" carried people away . . . according to thoroughly undocumented accounts.

Because of many years of hiking experience in the vast Pacific Northwest, my employers had hired me to do the job since I was familiar with almost every recess of the Manning Park wilderness region . . . in spite of the fact that I had never seen anything that even remotely resembled an ape-man. I had set up camp and begun my vigil on a slight rise above the lake on June 28.

And there I was. Unarmed. In Manning Park. At Nicomen Lake.

Surprised at the unexpected visit, I lay in the sleeping bag too long to take advantage of perhaps my only opportunity to see, and pop a flashbulb at, one of the rarest creatures on earth. Another loud clatter occurred when the brute kicked my pots and pans aside as he charged out of camp and vanished into the wailing forest. I wondered what on this planet could frighten a Bigfoot!

Now that the monster had fled the scene, I could hardly wait to pour plaster of Paris into his tracks to make castings. What if the downpour should wash away his footprints before dawn? Of course, I could have rushed out into the swirling storm and sprayed the prints with a waterproofing plastic compound I kept inside the tent, but I'm much braver in the light of day.

How well I remembered reading (long ago) the fearful tales of campers dragged from their sleeping bags at midnight, never heard from again. According to "reliable" sources, many hikers have never returned from those perilous regions. Who among big-game hunters had not heard the bloodcurdling roar of Sasquatch? But to my knowledge, nobody had ever spoken of any high-pitched mumblings like the sounds I heard during the time my "visitor" was in camp. Noise alone, however, was no real clue to Bigfoot.

Although serious danger accompanies every north-woods adventure, I've rarely found a logical reason to carry a firearm on any wilderness trip, particularly as a defense against an animal whose very existence is questionable. Even if I had a gun and met Sasquatch face to face, I would not shoot.

As the night wore on, a warm eastern wind swept the chinook's clouds from the clabbery sky. Silence and calm once more joined the brooding mystery of the Nicomen basin. The jagged Nicomen Ridge of tall peaks, where the main storm had raged, soon became muted of all sound. Time and a sky full of stars seemed purposely holding back the distant grin of dawn.

At graylight, before any color tinted the crests, I watched several owls move cautiously into what Cree Indians in Canada call predawn "owl-light."

When finally it became light enough to see, I made a quick inventory of the rucksack's contents. A Sierra Club cup, one package of mixed nuts, and a bar of soap were missing. Other utensils were on the ground beneath the pack. Had Sasquatch learned to drink from a tin cup . . .

14

had the giant ape learned to use soap? According to all reports, he was known to give off a highly offensive odor.

At sunrise I searched everywhere but found no Bigfoot tracks in the nearby mud. How could that horrible creature, weighing between 600 and 800 pounds, have paid me a midnight visit and escaped without leaving footprints in the gooey clay at the campsite? He could have taken the entire food supply, rucksack, packrack, and all. How come he didn't do any of that?

The next night I barely slept, because I was determined to get a flash picture if my visitor returned. At no time, however, was the peaceful evening disturbed by clattering utensils, mumblings, or other ruckus. Nevertheless, upon lowering the pack next morning, I discovered two neatly cut drawstrings. Packaged raisins, two chocolate bars, and my only fork had vanished. Probably filched while I dozed.

This time telltale tracks the size and shape of a human baby's hands left the clearest possible evidence in the mud: An exceptionally light-fingered raccoon was on the loose, testing no doubt the extent to which I would allow him to practice the burglar's nimble-handed trade.

One of the Northland's best climbers, his trick was to shinny up the tree, slip down the rope like a monkey, burglarize the rucksack, then escape with his loot. Raccoons have four "hands," twenty nimble fingers—adaptable as those of monkeys.

Then, on the morning of July 4, either the bandit's curiosity got the better of him or the smell of bacon and flapjacks simply defeated innate wild instincts. For whatever reason, I was able to talk a large male raccoon into camp—with the offer of half a pancake and on the condition that I move about on hands and knees. A person's upright position on two legs frightens most wildlings. Indians crawl on all fours when they wish to make friends with wild animals. A little skeptical about trusting me, he finally loped in with a rolling stride and sat down near the fire pit on a section someone had sawed from the huge fallen trunk of a hemlock. I called it Speculation Log. When serious thinking was required, it took place on that log. The raccoon's expression shone with intelligence and lack of anxiety. I felt pretty sure who the real Sasquatch was in these woods.

At first he bolted away, shrieked, and kicked up everything loose when I forgot to crawl around on hands and knees. He soon got over that.

Because of his boldness and sassy manners, I supposed earlier campers and fishermen had made his acquaintance, then pampered him with goodies. He had undoubtedly looked me over from some secret hiding place for several days to determine whether he could set me up as a sucker. Raccoons do that. Except for ground squirrels, chipmunks, and one moron marmot, local animals had avoided me at Nicomen Lake.

More or less convinced now that Sasquatch had *not* yet paid me a visit, I sat on Speculation Log to enjoy breakfast in that magnificent wonderland. As things worked out, however, the raccoon and I haunched at

16

opposite ends of the five-foot log. I clung to one rim of my aluminum plate. He seized the other side. We both pulled for all we were worth, grabbing bacon and pancake with as many fingers as possible, but his twenty had me bested. He could roll on his fanny, balance with his tail against the Log, hold my plate with his hind "fingers," and stuff his mouth with both front hands. Each glared at the other as a shameless glutton. How that nervy varmint could cram his face with grub—without bothering to chew! I was torn between two urges: to swat his fat rear end out of camp . . . or hug him. At the time I did neither. If a raccoon misinterprets your intentions, he can bite harder than a dog fox.

As we sat and scowled into one another's eyes after gobbling the breakfast, the raccoon pounded the Log with my plate, rippling enough high-pitched mumblings to remove the last doubt as to who had raided my supplies. At that very moment I recalled a notorious bad hombre from Tombstone, Arizona, by the name of John Ringo. While robbing banks and stage coaches in the 1870s, Ringo used to mumble in a high-pitched voice. It was a kind of trademark.

And that was how Ringo, the robber raccoon, got his name.

Comparing his personality with that of John Ringo, I cringed at the thought of hobnobbing for perhaps weeks with a scoundrel whose brassy life-style was 90 percent robbery. He faked a false, detached look while denting

17

the plate. A fraud to the core, he was clearly more hard-boiled than a picnic egg. Still, there appeared to be something mysterious about him, something I sort of half-liked.

A constant source of surprises filled the next three days. What would a lowlander raccoon be doing at 5,000 feet above sea level? Ringo's natural nighttime habits should have kept him dozing away the daylight hours in some small cavelike den or hollow tree in a nearby canyon at a much lower altitude. But here he was. He may have refused to sleep lately during the daytime for fear of missing something. He hung around my camp or hiked with me when I went for firewood or searched for Bigfoot tracks around the lake.

Even on his native soil, the raccoon seldom vacates marshside *coondominiums*—trees or caves—that house up to five families. Two or more couples may break away from a colony but travel less than a mile to establish a settlement of their own when their elders become cantankerous. Normal individuals seek lots of coonkind company. Therefore, Ringo's hermitage on a lonely lakeshore crawling with natural enemies, lacking his kind of food, providing little opportunity for the amount of mischief it takes to satisfy a raccoon's larcenous heart surprised me. Downstream from the lakeshore one distant marsh, one limited swamp, and one shallow creek offered little forage at great expense of time and effort.

Ringo was full of shockers. Atypical of raccoons, he washed no food in camp before eating, even with a

18

nearby basin of water. Only "wild" food—insects, mice, and berries—received a dunking in the lake. He used the basin for washing his hands up to twenty times a day! One could hardly believe this fussy oddball inhabited an evergreen forest instead of a nearby canyon. Big hollow cottonwoods in lower altitude valleys provided natural shelter that for some reason he scorned. I wondered whether he had perpetrated a problem at home resulting in expulsion. That happens among coons.

Looking closer at Ringo's occasional uptight behavior, I sensed that most of his hang-ups were simple exaggerations. Although British Columbia raccoons recognize danger in large predators, they ignore many birds, grazers, and human beings. Yet Ringo, who must have weighed about thirty-three pounds, lost his cool and dashed away, hissing and crying in abject terror when a blubbery, ten-pound marmot accepted my invitation to waddle into camp for cashews and raisins. Squeaky half-pound pikas on nearby rocks caused the raccoon to shake, moan, and burp like a mule eating barley every time they faked a charge in his direction. Somewhat later I discovered that Ringo was willing to pay a price for attention.

On the fifth day of our association, two musky little weasels and a marten chased the raccoon into the chilly lake. On the other hand, a seventy-five-pound beaver often buddied up to him for an amazing amount of chitchat and roughhousing at the pond in Nicomen Creek Canyon. They wallowed in the mud, wobbled

19

along the water's edge, and swam together in perfect harmony, two personalities poles apart. A varying hare—snob of the northwoods—not only allowed Ringo to groom his thick fur but also skipped, hopped, and jumped in circles when the indiscreet raccoon tried to probe the mysterious depths of the hare's long ears. They played "games" for hours. On several occasions Ringo tried to fool around with fawns, but does gave him the signal to keep "hands off."

His reactions to his Nicomen neighbors revealed a segment of his makeup related to understanding. On his black-masked face a kind of "guilty expression" appeared each time I bawled him out for outgrabbing me during a meal. He understood what I meant. He hung his head during my lecture when I caught him eating a killdeer's eggs. I suspect that his look of gloom may have reflected a reaction to the distress he saw in my eyes rather than any expression of conscience. Toward the end of that first week with him, as a means of self-defense, I stooped to barbarian tactics for the preservation of my food supply. I dusted his fat fanny with a switch. He learned fast.

Besides the time he devoted to his fellow creatures—and theft—Ringo satisfied his passion for taking things apart. He could unlatch, unbuckle, unzipper, or unhook anything from which I attempted to exclude him. Haunching often and clinging with the fingers of his hind feet, he applied his busy front fingers to projects that required the leverage of two hands: packages of dried food, pieces of collected loot, skins of fried trout, my lunch box, the lard can.

The extent to which those fingers were developed impressed me during his scrap with a local coyote on our first hike together to the far side of the lake. Ignoring the alpenstock I always carried for defense against big predators, the raccoon grabbed the ragged old song-dog, hung on with jaws like a bulldog, ripped flesh, and choked his opponent with the fastest and most efficient four hands in the North American wilds. His speed was hard to believe. I thought the aged coyote had thereby learned not to mess with Ringo, but he was not wounded enough for a lesson, as we realized later. Like raccoons, coyotes don't give up easily.

Not just during that first fight but also for the entire time we were together, I observed Ringo's use of intelligent strength, speed, and courage as his chief survival assets. Compared with most local animals, he was slow on his feet, yet he was a rapid galloper that no man could pass in a footrace. During a swim-bath in the lake where he swam circles around me, I recognized him as an aquatic mammal. Like his friend the beaver, he could dog-paddle and cut all sorts of monkeyshines at the same time. His species has been on earth 30 million years longer than man. Fast headwork and footwork, day or night life-style, and easy-to-please food habits have kept him from becoming extinct. Still individual raccoons rarely live longer than a dozen years.

As a result of our growing friendship, he practiced bold and swaggering bravado, especially after he found out how easy it was to bluff the marmot and pikas who had bluffed him. I filled a notebook with examples of Ringo's pretense. He was a walking handbook on self-educated trickery. But his real art was bald-faced theft. Noiselessly he five-fingered from every wild "collector" of food, shiny objects, and charms. For the most part he swiped useless articles for which he could not possibly invent a need. On each of our hikes into the forest, canyon, or upland meadows, I noticed that he was equally clever at lifting nuts, sun-ripened meat, slugs, fruit, and berries that his neighbors had spread to dry. For Ringo, stolen grub seemed to taste better than anything he had earned.

A few well-meaning people say animals don't really steal . . . they just take what they need. Would you hire the best-fed coyote, fox, or lynx to babysit the geese? Ringo was a thief to the core, but his hangdog facial expressions sometimes indicated that he might have experienced "feelings of guilt" for having committed specific crimes for which I shamed him. When I placed a cookie on Speculation Log and warned him to leave it alone, he would wait until I turned my back before stretching a slow and sneaky hand toward the goodie. As I whirled around, he quickly withdrew his sticky fingers, thus revealing one thing only: he respected the difference in our sizes. If, however, I allowed him enough time to filch the cookie and bite into it, he hung his head when caught in the act, looked pleadingly into my eyes, and chittered most appealingly—probably another of his artful dodges. He then handed me a *small fragment* of

the sweet, further proof that his greedy act was basic to an ancient law of survival. If I continued to shame him or give him the "silent treatment," he set in motion a series of ploys to regain my good graces . . . cuddled, churred softly, scratched my beard (instead of pulling it to elicit a threat), brought me a pinecone or a stink beetle. Like fishermen, he would trade a worm for a fish any day.

At this point I rather suspected him of hatching some kind of overall plan. It was just a hunch, but he appeared capable of a slick trick.

During our next days together, my sneaking suspicion that his plan may have included my help in stealing from the glut of local wealth being harbored by neighbors too big, fast, and dangerous for a raccoon's tricks increased. He had set his grasping heart on nest ornaments of local crows and ravens: tableware, keys, foil, ball-points, sun-glasses, bottle caps—loot that the birds had pirated from campers in the Similkameen River valley. Ringo cased his marks for days before pulling a job—a further illustration of a "thinking" animal. Primitive, yes, but a big first step.

Born kleptos themselves, crows, ravens, foxes, and pack rats pinched glittery plunder wherever they found it because of its attractive dazzle at the moment of theft. By contrast, I believed that Ringo was a bold and prissy thief who stole only after careful study of specific loot with intense prior observation of the owners. I never saw him shoplift any hardware that required little or no "art." After ten days I assumed that he stole for the sake of stealing.

Observation of details convinced me that the raccoon harbored a secret but impelling and exciting plan or drive that he was about to share with me. I sensed further that his feelings for me were now somewhat spliced into this mysterious eagerness to accomplish a stealthy goal. During those early days of relatively peaceful summer inactivity, he had laid some rather subtle groundwork.

2

The Rogue of Nicomen Lake

IN addition to petty thievery and downright burglary, Ringo had mastered the pickpocket's craft. Five times I felt light-fingered hands deep inside my pockets where attractive loot rattled. He not only pinched and hid items of my property that I neglected to *coonproof,* but also spent thoughtful hours planning visits to distant parts of the basin in the safety of my company . . . for the purpose of looting the less gifted. I soon grew to love that wretch in spite of his hateful art. Eventually he seemed to lead me wherever he wanted to go.

When not actively engaged in other adventure during that week of July 10, the busy rascal climbed a tall lodgepole pine ostensibly to enjoy the view. What he viewed with such delight was a gaudy collection of shiny treasures that adorned a crow's nest in the next tree. The huge loosely woven roost belonged to a sticky-beaked crow whom I called Epoxy. Every portable object not tied down seemed to glue itself to that crow's beak. When Ringo climbed down and shuffled back to camp, he was probably analyzing strategy through several options open to him. I knew something was up when he began avoiding my eyes during meals on Speculation Log. He stroked his whiskers, then examined his nimble fingers and itchy palms, but he kept his gaze down even when I spoke to him or offered him a goodie. Close cuddling was supposed to answer my queries.

However, he was hardly more of a rogue than the creatures from whom he stole. Long before that summer at Nicomen Lake, I became convinced that many wildlings often hustle one another's belongings as a primitive means to impress a prospective mate. Many animals love to test sharp-witted abilities and sticky fingers, a method of showing off by both sexes. Boldness, as a trait or as educated know-how, has enormous survival worth in practical and psychological ways. Ringo apparently had no mate to impress.

Late on the afternoon of July 12 I watched through binoculars as my friend shinnied up the tree to the unoccupied crow's nest. The robber lifted as many bright objects with boondocks value as he could carry to a small cave at the outlet end of Nicomen Lake. He returned to my campfire, climbed the Log, sat down beside me, and looked me squarely in the eye with an expression of open-faced innocence like a newborn fawn.

After dark he loped back to his cave to enjoy the rewards of his shrewdness. His natural night vision almost equaled his ability to see in the light of day.

Because some informer in our basin had pointed an

identifying paw, talon, or hoof, the voicy crow popula-
tion spent July 13 in awesome revenge. They chased him
up and down the lakeshore and finally drove him into the
forest. The weak link in his getaway had been his failure
to recognize how closely that flock of crows cooperated.
After relaying the emergency calls from family to family,
the birds formed fighter squadrons with a grudge. How
an infuriated crow can peck!

When at last his embarrassment and aching hips
brought him to seek refuge on my lap at Speculation
Log, his broad bottom and back—undoubtedly aching
more than his conscience—bristled with beak welts. He
sat and watched Epoxy and her mate Moxy, as they
returned loot to the empty nest. As might be expected
after they repossessed their own property, the crows
took a heavy penalty in the form of other victims' booty,
which they filched from Ringo's well-stocked cave.

The raccoon's failure seemed to stick in his gizzard.
He moped and grumbled for the rest of the day, but I
refused to play "good Uncle Bob." I knew better than to
laugh at him. Wild animals are extremely sensitive to the
human hee-haw. But he read the message in my eyes.

Killing time recovering from the beating the crows
had given him, Ringo squandered most of the fourteenth
as if he were simply loafing about camp. He soaked his
peck welts in the lake and killed endless hours staring
into space. In reality, from atop the Log he could check
out a family of "wealthy" red foxes in a nearby wild rose
thicket. The only creature in the woods able to outsmart

27

a fox is another fox. Through some strange mishap in judgment, Ringo decided to match wits with the slickest crooks that ever drew breath. The Nicomen Lake family of foxes had amassed a "fortune" in assorted wealth. Highly desirable rabbits' feet, glistening white wishbones from recently deceased geese, brilliantly colored teal wings, and a dried owl's foot represented but a small number of trophies that made Ringo drool.

Under cover of darkness that same night, the raccoon hid near the wild rose patch while the dog fox and his vixen hunted attractive loot. That intriguing couple rolled in wealth. They soon returned with golden squirrel tails and silver trout heads. Most unexpectedly they flushed Ringo near their den and chewed him without mercy because they suspected him of loitering and trespassing on their property for the purpose of stealing.

While crows continued to bad-mouth the raccoon on the sixteenth, his attention shifted toward his next project. The wily fox family habitually crawled from their thorny-fenced estate shortly before sunset each day in order to bathe before hunting—a foxy trick to eliminate their own smell, to put downwind prey at a disadvantage. The raccoon certainly knew his victims' habits, because he left my camp a quarter hour after the two foxes had snuck away for their evening chase. He must have known to the minute when they would return home. From a nearby tree he watched the pair climb to an alpine heath where they caught voles. The stealthy raccoon then slithered into the foxes' thorny corridor and cautiously crept toward the den's cluttered opening.

There he selected several family trophies, including the much-coveted dried owl's foot. But once again, he made a mistake in spite of clever planning. He should have emulated the foxes and bathed before raiding their den. He misjudged a fox's tracking nose—one of the most sensitive to faint odors in the animal kingdom.

Unintentionally Ringo left a scent trail to the very opening of his treasure cave. The foxes tracked him as easily as they would have followed an elephant in the snow.

Before punishing him for his crime, they muscled him out of their property (and some of his own), which they carried home—a distance of almost a mile. The next morning they skipped their customary habit of dozing away the daylight hours in order to enjoy what must have been to them a more satisfying sport. The couple whipped the burglar for half a day with every known means of torture they could muster. They prevented the raccoon from climbing trees, entering my camp, or dashing into the lake. They barred every avenue of escape because they were at least three times as fast as he was. Then he panicked. No sooner would the vixen block his way and box his jaws, than the dog fox would rush in for a chunk of coonskin. Wherever the burglar turned, he found himself nipped from the opposite direction. No *single* fox could outfox an adult raccoon in a fair scrap, but a cooperating pair might eventually inflict serious wounds. So, I finally went to his rescue. The foxes had made their point. They retired to their covert.

The raccoon dragged back to camp to lick his bruised

and bloody hide, refusing every goodie I offered him. He turned his head to avoid my eye. At about sundown he headed for his pillaged cave near the lake's outlet.

On the eighteenth he finally came back to my campsite, crankier than a goose penned up with a flock of ducks. Unfinished business occupied much of his concentration. He paced back and forth in front of me, at last tugging at the legs of my jeans. He clucked, churred, and mumbled in an attempt to enlist me as an accomplice in some kind of wilderness mugging. For a moment I hoped he had found a Bigfoot clue.

At two o'clock that afternoon I followed him to a pack rat's twiggy dwelling. The rodents skedaddled because raccoons think fat pack rats are delicious. Then, without my help, it took him more than an hour of hard labor to tear down one pack rat's home.

Without ceremony he proceeded to demolish other pack rats' wigwams—each three feet high, three feet in diameter. When nothing remained of each dwelling except the parlor, Ringo stepped in and collected the family loot comprised of jewelry, coins, tableware, fancy spinners, expensive glasses, film cartridges, pens, a pair of scissors, and one Timex—swiped from campers and backpackers. The raccoon left behind such trifles as foil, plastics, bottle caps, empty cartridge shells, and nails. Something told me he had looted pack rats' dens before, given that he knew the care he had to take with devil's-claw, a native shrub whose small branches bristled with sharp thorns. Many rodents weave devil's-claw into their structures to discourage thugs like Ringo.

Twice the heartless villain skittered along the beach to his den where he stacked his new wealth.

Quite unexpectedly an amazing drama occurred. I sensed big trouble when seven adult rats left the area together and headed deep into the forest. Within half an hour battle-crying pack rats appeared to sprout from every clump of underbrush—a brown swarm of two dozen, one-pound, bushy-tailed trade rats hotly chased the raccoon to the lakeshore about fifty yards from camp. Somehow he knew better than to jump in the water. Pack rats can swim as well as raccoons. That angry wave of rodents yearned to gnaw the robber's hide. No use climbing a tree; that would be fatal, because the rats could also climb.

His next move may have been coincidence. I have no

way of knowing to this day if he intentionally led his would-be lynchers directly beneath a dead cottonwood where lazy goshawks, red-tailed hawks, and great horned owls waited before looking for an evening meal. Instantly the drowsing birds sprang to life and dove into the ranks of squealing rodents, accordingly rescuing the thief from his pursuers. Although no one can say with certainty that Ringo deliberately Pied-Pipered the rats into the trap, the results were the same.

Apparently enjoying at least that one coup of successful banditry, Ringo spent much of the next few days in the plentiful berry and mushroom crop on the slopes above the marsh not far from the lake's outlet. On July 21 two female bears with four cubs and two yearling hangers-on took over the upland meadows. When eight bears of any kind move in, every other form of animal life generally moves out. Mother bears tolerate no help from father bears when it comes to raising the young. They dislike company of all kinds. According to internal clocks, midsummer launched that wonderful annual treat of getting fat on a diet of berries, mushrooms, grubs, small rodents, and huge slimy wood slugs. When food sources became exhausted toward the end of July, the bears would chase away sheep, deer, and wapiti to graze on the higher grassy berms just like hoofed animals.

That husky family in question held onto one—and *only* one—material possession: a sweet arbutus burl, round and about the size of a softball. Jealously guarded or carried day and night by the two nomad families even when they foraged, the burl was lovingly hugged, pawed, licked, gnawed, rolled, and shared. At least one bear remained at all times within swat range of the highly favored hardwood charm.

From a safe distance the well-hidden Ringo eyed the bears . . . *and the burl!* I prepared to kiss him good-bye. To pinch that souvenir would demand the most delicately organized and scheming skill he had ever employed. Within the raccoon's mind such a trophy must have mushroomed in importance.

As a species, bears are among the most respected woodland dwellers. They ask only to be left alone. With fantastic skill in the use of the brawniest swat in the animal kingdom, they *demand* to be left alone. Because men—and a few women—have hunted bears for ridiculous bearskin rugs, the species looks upon people as a kind of permanent target for revenge.

On the withering afternoon of July 21, the air temperature throughout the sprawling wilderness must have topped 100° F. By that date Ringo probably believed that my rock-throwing arm would defend him when enemies overtook him or badly outnumbered or outweighed him. I refused to allow Moxy and Epoxy or their raven cousins to peck him after that one generous thrashing. A swift look was generally enough to advise foxes or soberfaced owls that Ringo's fanny was off limits unless he had committed a theft causing them loss of

33

food or property. Hence, the raccoon rarely ventured out of sight or calling distance if he anticipated any need for his backup man. By then, however, I believe he recognized my disapproval of certain thefts and other equally foul deeds that curdled his welcome among our neighbors.

Unable to locate the mischievous varmint on that sizzling afternoon, I rather suspected an outbreak of hanky-panky. He had been so very tender and cuddly . . . questionably so, that day in particular.

At first I imagined that he was either flaking out in his own cool den, polliwogging in the shady marsh, or berrying on the breezy hillside. I should have admitted to myself that he was never too sleepy, too hungry, or too busy to skip a promising adventure. As he skittered about, shedding his summer coat, he looked for all the world like a miniature ragged bum.

Suddenly recalling his observation of the bears on the meadow, I scooped up the binoculars, grabbed the alpenstock, climbed the steep hill south of the lake, and scanned the grassland where I expected to find the browsing bruins. From the hilltop meadow I focused upon eight mounds of black fur sprawled out in a circle: siesta time in the lacy shade of an aspen thicket. A colony of bears has no enemy to elude in regions like Manning Park where hunting is prohibited.

Like a king-sized lollipop, the well-gnawed arbutus burl glistened in plain sight inside the family circle, near the larger granny bear. Because of her disposition I called her Old Mrs. Dynamite.

34

And there in thick grass, just outside the circle, crept grubby little Ringo. Compared to those mountains of muscle, he resembled a whippet among elephants. He seemed even tinier as he tiptoed silently through dry fodder. One smack from either one of those females would have wasted the raccoon. But he inched more and more slowly toward that exciting burl. My heart made an almost successful jump toward my open mouth when the rascal hopscotched into the circle of bears. As slowly as a serpent, he reached forward and carefully picked up the grand prize with his mouth. The sluggish bears slept as if drugged, while that slippery crook made a silent getaway.

The burl securely clamped between his jaws, he scooted across the meadow, down the hillside, and along

the lakeshore. At full speed he disappeared into his cave near the outlet (northwest end) of Nicomen Lake.

Hoping to be out of sight when the eight bears awoke and found their charm missing, I dusted gravel back to camp. Surprised at my hurry on such a hot day, mother deer and elk shook their heads then continued to teach their skinny-shanked fawns to graze the upland flats above the lake. A colony of marmots whistled their denunciation as I bounded over their burrows. Austere pikas stared in silence. I took advantage of every short-cut, not even pausing to admire a hillside blanket of fragrant glacier lilies whose yellow bonnets seemed to reflect the warm sunlight back into the sky.

Having climbed the first available lodgepole pine a short distance from camp, I held my breath as eight bellowing titans plunged wildly down the fragrant lily slope like rolling black boulders. Once on flat ground at the south end of the lake, they headed straight for my campsite. With both legs wrapped around the skimpy trunk, I grasped the sturdy alpenstock with both hands and made ready to contend with one beast at a time in the slender tree rather than face all eight at once on the ground.

3

Demons in the Bushes

HISSING and bellowing, the bears didn't even slow down when they scuttled through camp and roared along the sandy beach toward the outlet of the lake. I still embraced the lodgepole trunk.

Poor little Ringo! I swallowed a lump in my throat when I thought how much I would miss him.

Like raccoons and foxes, bears have a reputation for high intelligence. They may have known all along where the little pest denned up. Probably saw him casing that burl. They knew just where to look for it. One bear could rip the raccoon's bedroom apart in less than half a minute and grind him into *coonburger* meat in the bargain. Even if Ringo didn't take refuge in his den, it would be virtually impossible for him to hide from noses capable of sniffing him out wherever he went.

Bears can run, climb, dig, and swim faster than most North American species. But with all their great physical superiority, black bears rarely attack other animals except to punish an offense. They prefer carrion to live prey.

When Ringo saw himself trapped in his own den without possibility of escape, he rolled the magic burl out toward the beach. The Alpha (leader) bear, Old Mrs. Dynamite, quickly seized the wooden burl between her jaws, turned, and galloped quietly back toward the meadow napping-ground. The seven that turned and followed her looked arear several times toward the raccoon's quarters and rumbled about what could happen if that sharpy ever again took it into his evil head to cop their fragrant burl. The bears probably considered Ringo unworthy of a good thrashing on such a hot day.

When I knew Ringo better, I believed that he had peacefully surrendered the burl not only through fear of violent consequences but also because he had gotten all his kicks from the successful theft. The very act of lifting it from under the bears' noses had given him the boost he needed following his embarrassment at the mouths of crows and foxes. To Ringo the burl no longer represented the impossible. The tough wooden knot had lost its supreme value. Other matters now occupied his mind: I suspected some bigger business, unknown to me except as a vague supposition. His secret.

A riddle from his past seemed to occupy a big chunk of his time. Something seemed to haunt him, gnawing continuously at his peace of mind, goading him when he should have been relaxing.

For several days following the *one-coon* crime wave, Ringo made it clear that he was after my attention. He tried his best to express a message.

On the afternoon of July 26, he churred and whined, pulled the legs of my Levis, and sifted me through his eyes. When he thought I was furthest from getting his message, he bounced up and down in front of me like a yo-yo and shrieked like a monkey. When he was sure that I was honestly trying to separate fraud from frankness in his request, he mumbled and gently tugged at the hair on my arm. I felt ashamed of myself after having shaken an accusing finger at him and shouted that he deserved my distrust. But he failed to make me understand his lingo. At that time I could not guess what bothered him. I had to give up.

For fear that his mumbling had to do with food and that he might not be getting enough to eat on his own skimpy forage range, for at least a few days I fried a small cornmeal flapjack for him: *coonbread*. I caught extra trout and shared freeze-dried entrees with him. He never grew tired of trout, raw or cooked, but he preferred it cooked. Not a finicky eater, he gobbled everything I offered him. Our mutual sin was candy. He must have suffered the same high-altitude need for sugar that I did. Every time I broke out a candy bar, I believe we went through the same argument: Why the dickens should a two-legger on the basis of weight alone get two-thirds of the goodie? Then followed a spectacular display of the powerful, silent language of gestures and optical expressions. Where we had both failed before to convey a message, we now allowed our eyes to communicate. We enjoyed better success through what we could "say" with our eyes.

With a full belly on July 27, Ringo insisted that I accompany him down to the lakeshore. Able at last to decode that part of his message, I picked up the alpenstock and jogged along behind him.

He stopped and churred at the end of short bounds across the moist sand, clapping his "hands" to show his excitement that at long last I understood a trifle of his jabbering and optical expressions. Finally he led me to his summer den, a small cave near the lake's outlet less than a mile from my campsite. Through binoculars I had already discovered where his den was, but I didn't let on that I knew. The miniature chamber served as a snug, moss-lined, natural retreat near the base of a granite cliff three feet above high-water level. Yearling bear tracks still imprinted the moist sand in front of the den. Angry young bruins may have returned during the night or the cool of the afternoon to belt him a few just to let him know exactly where he stood. Lucky for him that he had spent the time with me, but then I feared the bears might also consider me his accomplice, guilty through association.

Crows, foxes, pack rats, and a host of unknowns had crisscrossed the threshold in front of Ringo's den. The footprints showed plainly enough that the little humbug had certainly earned the slurs of his neighbors. An entire community had beaten a path to his doorstep with hopes of recovering stolen property. If there was another reason for so much spoor, I was too slow to get it.

Ringo voiced no objections when I reached into his

"studio" and reclaimed my cup, fork, ball-point, pot lid, pocketknife, tent stake, Super-Duper spinner, coins, and safety pins. He may have tried to wash my soap. At any rate, the Lava, along with several items of food, had disappeared. I was more amused than angry at his indignant attitude. At length he seemed to shrug his shoulders with the message: "Everybody else has gotten his or her property back. You may as well have yours!"

Strange indeed was the discovery that no other animal had shared his retreat. Except for hardware "borrowed" from my pack rack, there were no items that he could have filched from other recent campers. That single fact may have contained a clue to Ringo's mysterious presence at Nicomen Lake. Had he not been an outcast from a colony, there would have been signs of at least one other raccoon near the den.

Sitting beside him and studying his constantly changing facial expressions, I racked my brain trying to discover the problem that seemed to torture him . . . and the role he planned for me to play. Was he an outcast really—one who dared not return to his colony? Nicomen Lake was *not* raccoon territory, not by any stretch of the imagination. From South America to British Columbia raccoons are *lowlanders,* not *highlanders.* It seemed reasonable to suppose that he had been expelled earlier that summer from a colony for bad conduct: murder, serious theft from other raccoons, dirty fighting with an inferior rival, laziness, or general meanness. Those are the usual crimes for which fellow coons get the

41

boot. I had no way of proving my theory. Exile to a hostile territory, such as Nicomen Lake basin, a land of husky predators, defeating weather, and starvation diet, meant almost certain death before September's Moon-of-Painted-Leaves—not to dwell upon the six succeeding months, known to Indians as Hunger Moons. Come January's Moon-of-the-Storm-King, up to fifty feet of snow would cover the level areas, much deeper in drifts. Without one hollow tree or log within miles, Ringo had no den in which to nap out Cascade winter storms. That damp and drafty cave would kill him. Within less than a minute any big predator could root him out. Raccoons don't hibernate in the true sense of deep stupor and lowered metabolism.

His solitary presence at lonely Nicomen Lake had puzzled me from the beginning of our friendship. In the first place, it made no biological sense that an intelligent wild animal with normal ability to survive would enlist a human being for an ally. Raccoons often join up with other mammals for what is known among ecologists as *symbiosis:* mutual effort toward mutual benefit . . . but not with people. A crow leads a fox to a rabbit warren. The fox kills two rabbits: both crow and fox feast. A coyote makes a deal with a badger. The coyote, a faster mammal, herds mice into the badger's burrow. The fox shares rabbits, the badger shares mice: symbiosis.

For a time I strongly suspected that Ringo had been human raised, later cast aside, as so frequently happens to baby wildlings adopted as "pets." Alone he faced not only his mysterious conflict with himself but also impossible problems with that harsh region of knify winds, deep-freeze winters, starvation, and predators. Moreover, like all raccoons, he hated solitude. A human being was his only answer.

You would have to know the silence, loneliness, and remoteness of Nicomen Lake honestly to understand the situation in which Ringo found himself. He was clever enough to recognize his problem. And so, he grabbed onto a human companion, a man whom he correctly analyzed as a soft touch, one upon whom he could comfortably rely and often boss around. Strange how they know, but they do!

After that confidential get-together at his den, we became solid sidekicks. He never again pinched my supplies or equipment. His table etiquette did not improve visibly, although he tested to his own satisfaction what bad conduct I sometimes tolerated at the Log. He seemed to reveal that he was now willing to put everything he had into true friendship, and I began honestly to love the critter.

In order to prevent dependence upon me as a temporary or artificial food source, I mustered all my willpower and shared fewer chocolate bars and *coonbread* with him. Unwise human association could have deprived him of natural ability to survive when the human left. Freeloading on my "doggy-bag" leftovers could have caused him to give up independent foraging. Dependence upon human protection could have dulled his wisdom when it came to outwitting natural enemies.

43

Henceforth, with handouts cut to the core, we struggled together through every marshland bog and upland moor for natural raccoon food: insects, grubs, worms, tubers, berries, fungi, frogs, slugs, water snakes, seeds, fish, and carrion. Almost daily we walked through dense forest for morels, tender green shoots of vine maple, and salal berries.

While we collected Ringo's food items, my enthusiasm for finding Bigfoot clues definitely began to wane, the result of fruitless search through every biome in the region. Nevertheless, though it seemed hopeless, I continued exploration for a part of every day.

Almost as if he believed that each woodland sound and movement in the bush threatened him, Ringo also seemed to search at all times for monsters that did not exist. Whether danger loomed more in the imaginary state than in reality was beside the point. Fear of danger harried him, and the expression in his eyes occasionally accused me of having set him up for top-rung fright or traumatic shock each time we chanced upon fisher, coyote, or lynx. He never forgot the lifted eyebrows of my neutrality on the days I allowed crows, foxes, rats, and bears to humiliate him.

Despite any harbored grudges, he responded to affection and expected to receive it daily. It may be that he supposed I was there exclusively for his welfare. At any rate he learned to live with his anxieties through instinctive adjustments resulting from experiences, memory, and what he discovered to lean on. As a raccoon out of his natural region, he had seized upon me, a nonthreatening animal, and created a close bond: one that promised to assuage his fears and weather his storms. Regardless of motives and the fact that he was a pain in the neck on an almost daily basis, frankly I was flattered that a wild animal had adopted me for *any* reason.

Shortly after the arbutus burl fiasco, and while Ringo still smarted under four defeats, there occurred one of the strangest nonleaning alliances I have ever witnessed in the wilds. He took up with a porcupine whom I called Porky. And nobody leans on a porcupine.

The two animals appeared not to have known one another before I came to the lake. What they got from the association I'll never know. To my knowledge, it was in no way a symbiotic relationship. Raccoon and porcupine brains are in two different leagues. Their diets are in no way related. Ringo foraged marsh and meadow, while Porky girdled young pine trees in deep forest. Ringo had adjusted to daylight hours. Porky remained exclusively a night forager. He scowled at the world beneath a load of 30,000 barbed quills. His brain was on a par with that of most rodents—retarded. Ringo, on the other hand, possessed a sparkling personality—mischievous, outgoing, fun-loving, brainy. The only trait the two creatures had in common was size; each weighed about thirty-five pounds. Local meat-eaters were a mild threat to both animals, but no coyote, bobcat, or fisher was mentally soft to the extent that he would take on both buddies at the same time . . . and that may have sealed their friendship. When slowly the two strolled down the beach together, they never had to elbow their

way through any kind of crowd. Toward the end of July, I watched Porky and Ringo a lot. Their favorite get-together meant climbing a tree and sitting more or less side by side on a thick branch for an hour.

On each occasion I sat under the tree of their choice and listened without making a sound. What I heard was almost as strange as the fellowship itself: In tones not unlike background noises produced for effect on TV, both animals gurgled, mumbled, churred, spluttered, gibbered, and chomped their teeth at the same time. If such a racket were indeed friendly conversation, I should have dreaded the day when an *argument* might break out.

As Ringo and I hiked to different areas shortly before sunset every day in order to look for any signs of Sasquatch, we often found Porky in low bush at the edge of an aspen thicket. On those occasions Ringo became immediately serious. Porky was always serious. For a few minutes both animals sat down in order to resume—so it seemed—that endless debate in B-flat minor. They buzzed, hummed, and whined. Upon parting company with his advocate, Ringo appeared more alert, even jumpy . . . as if the two had agreed upon the deadliness of their enemies. The routine never changed.

Always tuned in on local jitters, I studied each condition to learn of any dangerous animal's visit. Should a Sasquatch appear, I would want to know the exact reactions of all species in the basin.

Of the raccoon's specific ogres—predators, competitors, and weather—nothing tormented him more than a hefty thunderstorm.

On the evening of July 30, just after sundown, mile-high thunderheads shoved their way in and began roughhousing around Three Brothers Peaks. The sky looked as if it were making room for a genuine gully-washer. I jogged down the lakeshore toward Ringo's den in order to reassure him during the bombardment, but the bounder met me halfway and indicated with optical expression that we should turn back and head for my tent, a drier bivouac. A hunting team of coyotes sang before the last light faded. We reached the tent in time.

As lightning activity increased, the smell of pinewood smoke permeated the bone-dry basin. We could not survive a severe forest fire.

4

Foul-weather Friends

WE had barely plunged into the pup tent when the first thunderblasts reverberated through the camp. Hot wind whipped the creaking forest and churned the lake. Dry bolts of lightning not only whittled at the distant Brothers Peaks but also splintered a nearby 200-year-old larch. What was left of the tree and several shrubs caught fire.

Although there were few conifers and underbrush near our side of the lake and none on the hilly east and south sides, westward toward the Similkameen River gorge the forest grew dense, loaded with pitch and turpentine. Pine, cedar, larch, hemlock, and fir. Charred logs throughout the area reminded me of killer blazes in the past. If fire didn't sizzle the meat off our bones, smoke could suffocate us within a mile of any big burn. As forked lightning struck nearby, setting new fires, and thunder exploded, the raccoon and I went quietly schizo.

Until that afternoon I had zippered and tied the pup

tent's opening each day against Ringo's nimble fingers. But without other shelter when rain and hailstones began to pound the landscape, the emboldened scamp might have torn the tent in order to get inside. So, I left it unzipped thereafter. Then, too, I thought about Sasquatch, skunks, porcupines, and bears. Most animal species in the basin now regarded me as a kind of harmless nuisance in their wilderness world. They might enjoy the dry shelter of that tent. Sprawled out on the sleeping bag's luxurious surface, we watched a shower of hailstones that resembled small ice cubes. Ringo, a perpetual wader who splashed into the lake, pond, or stream at every opportunity and who loved to walk for hours in the water, considered himself mortally wounded if he got wet in a thundershower or happened to be tapped by a little hail.

Clucking like a setting hen, he cuddled close to my chest, wailing and burying his head during lightning

strikes and thunderblasts. He uttered high-key whines when the noisy storm bounced from peak to peak along Nicomen Ridge—gnashed his teeth and groaned as smoke from several fires began to choke us. At length a "goose-drownder" with twisting columns of rain threatened to flood the basin, but the downpour extinguished the fires.

Shaking as if in the throes of a chill, Ringo pleaded with lowered head, almost as if he were praying. He seemed to have reached a point of honest confession that he was genuinely ashamed of his fear.

About nine o'clock that evening the storm petered out. We crawled forth and shared a hot beanfest. Most of my meals were as tasteless as a blackboard eraser, but Ringo indicated by his appetite that my cooking was A-1 gourmet, a remarkable example, I thought, of raccoon ability as a con-artist.

When he slowly headed down the lakeshore toward his den, I followed. He was anything but eager to pass up a dry night inside a down sleeping bag. Clouds still sagged over the basin, so dark that I lost the silent Ringo every few yards. When I sat down and called him, he crawled onto my lap, gurgled, hunkered like a kitten, and put his arms around my waist. I melted. He slept with me inside the down bag from then on—muddy little hands and feet included.

Much as he enjoyed close physical contact—rubbing, scratching, hand-holding, and cuddling—he squirmed and voiced objection whenever I picked him up and carried him under my arm. Being picked up and carried in the "paws" of another animal may have impressed him as a form of defeat. Although he never raised any real dickens about it, I sensed and respected his feelings.

Once certain that he disliked my carrying him, I scooped him up in emergencies only. Frequently startled by sudden appearances of other animals, he scrambled up to my shoulders, straddled my neck, and choked me with his hind feet. With his "hands" he clung to my hair or my ears, and was fully delighted with top-deck security. In the absence of danger, he simply clung to my hair and jumped up and down on my shoulders.

The raccoon hitched rides part of the way as we continued to explore distant sections of the Nicomen region for evidence of Bigfoot. Free to bounce and goof off on my shoulders was somehow different from being carried. Fun for him, torture for me. He weighed about thirty-six pounds by the end of July.

You might say that I kept up the search for signs of the mystical monster because several sensationalist writers had published articles declaring that the ape-man *could possibly* exist under Pacific Northwest conditions if he were a *carnivorous* (meat-eating) ape. They believed that Bigfoot could survive provided he underwent false hibernation for a part of each winter like bears and raccoons. Reliable authorities on animal life strongly deny any possibility of such an existence. They remind us that scientists have found *no* records of hominid (manlike) apes in the Western Hemisphere. Some very convincing photos of the great ape have also received the scientific stamp of phony: posed pictures in rented or homemade costumes. Even Mr. Patterson's movie has not escaped accusation.

Despite all the scientific evidence and my own private opinions, my conscience demanded that I cover every possible square foot of the region I was paid to study. My employers would frown like losers upon any story of a robber raccoon offered as a substitute for plaster castings where the more glamorous Bigfoot had strolled.

Even devoted pro-Sasquatch fanatics have begun to think seriously in terms of scientific reasoning. No skeletons, no fossils, no remains of any kind have ever been recovered in districts of reported sightings. No Sasquatch has ever fallen before any hunter's gun.

For many years I have hiked the most remote parts of that wilderness without seeing so much as one footprint made by a Sasquatch. I was hired in spite of the strong points I made of these facts.

The very name, Sasquatch, was traced to French *voyageurs* who called Anglo-Saxons *Sassenach* (the word itself is Saxon). Mispronounced and misspelled, the noun at last joined backwoods dialect and grew into *Sasquatch*. Used at first to point out bearded English trappers, the word later referred only to the mythical ape-men of brash campfire visionaries.

By August 1 I had just about concluded that the big ape had evolved in trailside imaginations. Still, considering the sincerity of my employers, I was unwilling to put the charming myth permanently to sleep, so I extended my efforts. One isolated group of diehards still accepts the "miracle" that Sasquatch never allows *disbelievers* to see his footprints!

Because of a further extension of hours in my search for clues, the raccoon received extra forage time. When he stayed out late, he simply lifted the bottom seam of the tent's mosquito flap, stole inside as silently as a burglar while I slept, then scared the daylights out of me by cramming a twisting finger into my ear or by tweaking my nose. I warned him with a swat that the outrage could earn him a maple-stick paddling, but even if he got the message, he must have assumed that I would not carry out the threat. I endured those nights when he sneaked into the sleeping bag *without* warning . . . when twenty icy, wet, gooey, wiggly fingers and toes made mud prints up and down my naked back at midnight! On such occasions the clown tried my patience beyond the call of duty. Today I marvel that he did not receive an involuntary clobbering before I recovered my cool. His trust was elementary faith no one could possibly violate.

He never established to my satisfaction a bona fide reason for giving up his natural nighttime foraging, yet he may have done so because I had offered him food on the Log at the beginning of our association. Instinct is nature's most demanding principle: prime motivator that requires little or no thinking. To help the raccoon overcome instinctive feeding habits and eliminate all nocturnal foraging, the August nights at Nicomen Lake became cold, moist, and windy. The number of big predators increased. Food became scarce. A weatherproof tent, dry sleeping bag, and a warm bedfellow no doubt made more sense than big ugly prowlers and cold windy hunger. Perhaps the temptation of comfort at this point simply overcame the wrench of instinct.

At any rate, we left camp early each day so that he could have more hours rummaging for natural coon chow. Human goodies at Speculation Log had been reduced to an arbitrary minimum. One example of headwork was his daily plea that I follow him with the alpenstock while he foraged. If I tried to go without the sturdy stick, he would rush to where it leaned, knock it down, roll it around, and lick it. But he never learned to pick it up. He may have considered the heavy cane less a weapon than a hoisting bar for lifting him quickly to my shoulders when an enemy loomed.

While helping him find food, I had to admit to my own conscience that we had forged an unnatural man-raccoon partnership. As stormy weather increased during that first half of August, we became closer thunderstorm buddies—an unnatural association. We napped out showers and drippy fog. We shuddered out electrical squalls. On clear days after a period of foul weather, to make up for lost time, we hiked far afield, during which outings he pillaged winter stores of chipmunks and squirrels while I looked on. I lied to my conscience by insisting that nothing a man could do would alter the Earth Mother's way. Animals have robbed one another since the first specimens wiggled through the primordial ooze.

While coon-herding and searching for signs of the elusive simian, I watched vigilantly for Ringo's enemies, another unnatural act . . . it undermined his own innate watchfulness. During those first two weeks in August, I scribbled endless notes in my logbook, observations along the trails and in camp pertaining to the raccoon's behavior and habits: events that might explain an unnatural confederation between me and one of Mother Nature's scalawags.

On the afternoon of August 15 he had eaten his fill of mushrooms, frogs, berries, iris roots, and rodent-stored grain. He sat quietly with me on a decaying log in the canyon forest. How close he came to reading my thoughts by studying my eyes! As human eyes best reveal the silent human interior, so raccoon personality and feelings leak out through raccoon eyes. By means of the looks in our eyes, we both understood our responses and mutual affection. Consequently, he learned to lay it on pretty thick, especially when his own native food was scarce. On that day I believed he was very close to revealing the real secret behind his push.

During moments of reason, I respected him as a wild animal. I honestly did everything possible to prevent our partnership from having unfortunate effects upon his independence when the day of my departure would inevitably arrive. As I sat and wrote in my notebook, he brought me a mushroom, a wild onion bulb, a freshly slaughtered frog, a squirming water snake. His generosity may have expressed payment for my half of what he could have considered a symbiosis. The thought also crossed my mind that such gifts could have been "advances" against a future activity in which he had already selected the role I would play. I learned to cope with one truth: without unfair advantages, it would be difficult for a man to outsmart *Procyon lotor,* the raccoon, on his native ground.

Another thing about the truths of late summer: he taught me to hum softly with him his one "song," while by flashlight I searched his thick coat for "galloping dandruff" before allowing him in the sleeping bag. It never flashed across his mind that I performed the chore in *self-defense* when I killed his fleas and ticks. Except during bad weather, he most often drowned his parasites in the lake or suffocated them in dust or mud baths. I don't ever expect to know why he refused to go in the lake when it rained!

With the sleeping bag zippered for the night, he cuddled as close to my chest and belly as he could wedge his three-foot length, fully outstretched. He rarely moved until his alarm-clock mind let him know that dawn was at hand. The possibility of food and frenzied adventure was even more fun than the luxury of further cuddling— unless it was raining.

Regardless of hidden motives and love of luxury, he seemed to prize our friendship. Trust, companionship, and understanding added up to mutual respect and affection, a value with limitless rewards for both of us.

On August 16 I woke with a shock. During a carefree month and a half, I had blindly allowed an acute emergency to develop right under my nose.

56

5

To Weave a Rainbow

ORIGINALLY the Sasquatch enthusiasts had allowed me, at most, the month of July for making plaster of Paris castings if and when Mr. Bigfoot stumbled into the mud. Not only July but also half of August had disappeared. It suddenly struck me that my food supplies, like time, had also vanished. A single issue buffeted my conscience: How could I possibly go away and leave Ringo to face an unreckoned number of deadly enemies? Without my alpenstock, rock-throwing arm, bellowing voice, and physical presence, he would have faced disaster in a whirlwind of beaks, hoofs, fangs, and claws within a few days after I hit the trail. The witty little beggar had made an enormous nuisance of himself, and had leaned too heavily upon the temporary support of one man. Because of our fellowship (and my protection), he had no doubt become far more unseemly in the eyes of his neighbors than he would have on his own.

Yearning for action, an old fisher and an even older coyote had teamed up as unrelated predators do: senior

57

citizens of the wilderness on a coon hunt. That partnership represented a real threat to coons, marmots, porcupines, kids, lambs, and fawns. Deer and elk hated Ringo's guts for the pleasure he had taken in silent, rude appearances like a ghost to spook them. Rocky Mountain sheep had similar bones to pick with my friend. Without my help the raccoon would find all hoofed animals ready to gang up on him. For the winter at least, most bears that threatened the little stinker had shuffled beyond the mountain.

In addition to local animals with grudges to settle against the pixy, old King Winter would swoop down on him shortly. Therefore, on August 16 I had no choice but to hike out to the nearest town for supplies. I left all equipment in camp except the empty rucksack and pack-rack. I slipped away at 4:00 A.M., while the raccoon was still sacked out in the tent. By sunrise I was halfway down Heather Trail headed for the highway in the Similkameen River valley.

On Provincial Highway 3, a trucker honored my thumb all the way to the town of Princeton. A grocer filled the pack with staple supplies, topping it off with candy bars, nuts, raisins, and tidbits that my friend was sure to relish. After paying for the supplies, I telephoned the Southern California Sasquatch people about my lack of success so far. I got their permission to continue the search in the Nicomen region—at my own expense and with no salary for the next five or six weeks. Before very long I had thumbed another ride back to the trailhead, but the round trip kept me on the go for twenty-six hours. A mantle of hollow light cast by a three-quarter moon made the trail visible but no easier to climb. That confounded pack weighed more than fifty pounds.

Even before arriving in camp, I called Ringo, but he had vanished during my absence. It was barely 3:00 A.M. The trip back up that trail had bushed me to the marrow. As soon as I had strung the rucksack to a limb, I crawled into the tent. Not a sound. The air was frigid and dead. A ghostly fog blanketed the lake. Worried about the raccoon's safety, I fell into bottomless sleep from sheer fatigue.

I lay snoring away on my back shortly before daylight when a pair of savage hands seized my ears and pinned my head to the floor of the tent. Heavy stomping feet began to jump up and down on my stomach and chest.

Even under such physical torture, I had difficulty waking up. Self-defense was out of the question anyway. I was unable to move no matter how hard I struggled to turn over. The animal's stinking body made me sick.

When the tent and the raccoon finally came into proper focus, I shouted at the top of my lungs, "Ringo, you varmint! If you ever do that again, so help me, I'll wring your ruddy neck and skin you alive!"

The fraud gently encircled my neck with his arms, clasped his fingers for a throttling hug. He licked me across the mouth and nose, while I skirmished with my conscience to keep from forgiving him for that awful nightmare. Then I laughed until tears ran down my face. I'm sure he laughed too—in his own way. We ran up a

fantastic number of hours laughing that summer away.

Daylight revealed plainly that my return as such had triggered his volcanic display of affection. There was an enormous chestnut to pull from the fire. Barely beyond my ammunition dump (a neatly stacked pile of throwing-sized rocks), a pack of seven coyotes shuttled silently around the campsite. While I was away, Ringo had probably spent much of his time warming the highest lodgepole or fir branch. One coyote *alone* would hesitate to take on an adult boar raccoon in prime shape. But seven could turn big Ringo into a tasty banquet.

A thin whine in the key of high-C summoned my attention to a sturdy lodgepole pine behind the tent. Because of fatigue and sleepy eyes, I was unaware that a full-blown crisis existed to explain the coyote pack in camp. Within moments the violin whine was repeated. I crawled from the tent. The seven coyotes froze in their tracks and snarled. A careful scan of the "whining" pine revealed two beady little eyes peering down from a branch about a third of the way up the trunk.

Impossible! A five-pound cub in a tree? No *adult* coyote could climb a tree, let alone a cub . . . unless the cub had been *assisted* by one thirty-six-pound raccoon!

It took less than five minutes to shinny up the tree trunk, grab the hissing, biting, clawing cub, then return the ill-tempered little brat to her mother.

Ringo, the "cubnapper"—looking nowhere but straight down—sat in the tent doorway manicuring his fingernails.

It occurred to me that the irate coyotes should have left as soon as their cub was reunited with her mother. But they trotted nervously around the campsite at a distance of less than fifty feet. Ringo shadowed my heels every step I took until after breakfast. When it was safe to do so, he scooted up the nearest tree. Armed with half a dozen polished rocks, I singled out what appeared to be the oldest, slowest, and most infuriated male coyote in the pack—probably the cub's granddaddy. Charging unexpectedly and with all my strength, I caught him off guard for a moment and pelted him until he yelped out of range. The pack retired—temporarily—down Heather Trail toward the Similkameen Valley.

I still wonder what mechanics Ringo used to boost that coyote up the tree. I suspect that he grabbed the little scamp by the nape of the neck and carried her in his mouth exactly as her mother might have done on level ground. He had four hands for climbing.

Even with the coyote pack elsewhere for the moment, fear still plagued Ringo. Of an evening when other ani-

61

mals prowled about the perimeter of our campfire light, his hackles rose and fell continuously. Tones of terror crept into his whisper. Like his eyesight and sense of smell, his hearing was remarkable. As a recognized fact, animals with the keenest senses are often "psyched out" by acute sensitivity to fear. A frightened animal, like a threatened animal, lives longest: He is the most careful one. Bears, with the sharpest sense of smell of all North American land animals, run from the urine posts of a fox terrier. Although Ringo clung to my heels, he shuddered whenever we crossed any path where wolverine, fisher, or marten had deposited a little musk. His startled cry quaked with dread each dusk when great gray owls booed our presence from overhead branches.

In any wilderness a patrol of raccoons could withstand almost any likely attack. Forty-pound males inflict mortal wounds on coonhounds foolish enough to engage even small family troops. A pair of raccoons has been known to band together with other pairs in order to waylay and kill a raiding cougar. Pound for pound, the wolverine is the world's strongest and fiercest land animal; yet the dreadful beast avoids contests with raccoons of equal weight. Northern woodsmen report that mother raccoons defending their young have killed lynx whose greater muscles, claws, teeth, and weight under other circumstances would have killed instantly any female raccoon.

In order to maintain optimum physical shape for fighting emergencies, Ringo practiced a routine of vigorous exercises. Only a fisher could outclimb him. Only otters

62

and beavers could outswim him. He practiced excellent health habits such as regular bathing, balanced diet, and rest. Each morning, like bobcats and cougars, he hiked to the nearest running water for his toilet. Of course, he was careful to wash his face and hands *upstream* from where he had just expelled body waste. As colony animals, raccoons of all ages seem to spend an inordinate amount of time in group activities such as bathing, wrestling, and running, practiced apparently for physical improvement.

In addition to his talent for "loner" mischief, Ringo possessed and often used the smooth-functioning kennel strategy of a colony member. He even exercised the good manners known to exist among family groups of the species. He licked my hand to show appreciation for special food goodies. He would mooch certain irresistible foods and often just grabbed others from my hands; yet when I fished, he never jumped into the water to seize a trout on the hook. As a hiker he was tireless, yet he never urged me on when I stopped to get my breath. Through personal decorum he displayed patience and concession. In the right frame of mind, he could be the most dazzlingly genteel wild animal I have ever known. Therefore, I was inclined to overlook much of his mischief and plain dirty tricks. Without jeopardizing any of his wildness, I regarded it as a duty to make life as much fun as possible for him.

From August 20 I referred in my notebook to certain highlights of our daily forage walks and Bigfoot scouting as "weaving a rainbow," a figure of speech—a Texas hyperbole if you like—that requires definition. For example, we both got genuine pleasure from the smell of warm forest duff in combination with edible fungi, sugary berries, or fragrant lilies. He sniffed the lily because he enjoyed the perfume; a built-in celebration of delight because it represented nothing in his diet. We paused and watched an eagle cling motionless to the edge of a cloud then hurtle from the sky toward prey with pinpoint accuracy. While predators slept, the drowsy-faced raccoon and I rolled in the last summer bouquets of wintergreen and bee-mint. We had a ball in the physical sense with our environment without taking anything . . . together we wove a rainbow of sheer ecstasy.

Instinct led him to link survival with habits of proven worth. Intellect *beyond* instinct tided him over in a region of changing needs and conditions. He faced the frightful backfires of his robbery failures but made no outwardly visible changes because of them. By all odds his best example of intellect under changing conditions was, of course, his choice of a human defender. It was not impossible that he had known another human being, but the better I knew him the more I doubted it. He had the brain power to recognize that his fort was under-manned against a bevy of the world's fastest and deadliest hunters of tasty raccoon flesh. With good-natured hums and bad-breath kisses, he honored me with genuine affection in return for the security he sensed in our association. New experiments requiring intelligent planning were always costlier—but were biologically more valuable—than reactions to raw instincts.

Perhaps half-instinct, half-thought, his moods—fresh, varied, and most often surprising—also followed consistent patterns. He was as cranky as a caged lynx after the failure of a theft; he celebrated every successful pinch with hummed joy. Whether seriously gathering food, swiping something from an animal neighbor, or just committing plain devilment, he acted in dead earnest. When keyed up by success, he geysered his happy feelings and danced around like a child. When down in the dumps because of a failure, he really scraped bottom. He sometimes looked glum and miserable, as if homesick for his peers. Thus, his reactions reflected both intellect and instinct. By the end of August he knew me well enough for deep confidences. He was no longer ashamed to "weep" in his own way. So, all of that—and more—was what it took to "weave a rainbow."

While the raccoon and I toyed with the dream-fabrics of rainbows and more or less thumbed our noses at apprehension, Old Jack Frost sneaked into our basin on the night of August 21 with his magic paints and brushes. During the last week in August, every alpine meadow above timberline wore a colorful autumn wardrobe.

Cold weather came early to the shores of Nicomen Lake. The chill of night began to carry over into the day. By September 1, our dreamy hikes and lazy hours of close companionship (and rainbow-hued moods) slipped unavoidably under the clouds of an unwelcome truth: The flinty edges of reality had cut into our fabric of fancy and fun. The search for a suitable den in which Ringo could sleep out the winter storms became more urgent as each item of his native diet disappeared because of the rapidly advancing season. Big lanky predators had also begun to feel the pinch of hunger. Lynx, wolverine, and cougar now seriously stalked warm coon meat. There were times when the killers all but ignored human presence until my war whoop and stony artillery went into action. Ringo reached my shoulders by clinging to the alpenstock and vaulting like a pole-vaulter. His contribution to our defense system was confined to hissing and shaking one "fist" then the other. Of a morning he sniffed a network of big pawprints in the moist earth at the very opening of the pup tent. Many the steamy warm breath near my head beside the mosquito flap

caused both of us to shiver; but when daylight came, all menace of nighttime disappeared . . . the sheep fears no wolf it cannot see. Our life-style, predicated upon woven rainbows at this stage, reminded me of Ralph Hodgson's beautiful couplet:

> *God loves an idle rainbow*
> *No less than labouring seas.*

Shortly before noon on September 2, the two of us were idling along, overturning a stone here and there in search of water bugs and hellgrammites in Nicomen Creek Canyon, half a mile below the lake's outlet. Ringo looked as if he were about to divulge his big secret. He began to churr in the most confidential manner. Maybe he would lead me to a distant colony of his brethren. At that precise moment, a movement, as slight as that of a frost crystal falling from an overhead leaf, flagged my attention. Directly above our heads, on a boulder not six feet away, crouched a hungry tom lynx about to spring.

6

Fangs in the Shadows

UNAWARE that I had seen the bloodthirsty beast, Ringo froze and sirened his alarm in concert with a whiskey-jack's warning whistle. The raccoon seemed to believe that meat-eaters posed the same threat to me that they did to him. His outcry may have meant that he was simply bawling me out for lousy vigilance. The lynx's stalk had been as silent as thought.

When the rangy ruffian arched to launch a spring against my friend, I hurled a rock with all my strength and hollered like Geronimo's ghost. The missile thudded off the big cat's rib cage. Screaming a combined yelp and wail that would have chilled Dracula's blood, the long-legged lynx leaped about three feet straight up. I readied my sturdy walkingstick for his charge, knowing full well that I could create at best no more than a minor nuisance as far as that predator's lunge was concerned. Fortunately for both of us, the cat changed his mind about an attack. He corkscrewed twice and bounded from the canyon. But the haunting incident proved that "rainbow-weaving" had indeed come to an end for man and raccoon. Another close shave like that—so I felt as I stood there and trembled—and I would die of a heart attack, right along with the quaking Ringo.

Believing himself camouflaged against autumn's carnival of colors in dense salal, vine-maple, sumac, and maple shrubs, the lynx had padded noiselessly as he approached the boulder, a planned encounter. With more than enough strength to kill a yearling deer, lamb, or mountain goat, the big predator could easily have broken Ringo's neck and dealt me a serious patch-up job at the same time. From that boulder the forty-five-pound lynx had more advantage than he realized. The whiskey-jack (Clark's nutcracker or camp robber) on an overhead branch had trumpeted the "lynx alarm" when the hefty beast arched for a pounce. Unfortunately for prey species, whiskey-jacks are not always at the scene to whistle warnings. Depending upon the extent of their hunger, the presence of man, or the poverty of a specific season, most northwoods predators roam night or day, taking only the old, wounded, stupid, careless, or excess young.

Whether reporting the presence of a killer or just shrieking to create an impression, whiskey-jacks are the noisiest early-dawn alarm clocks in the northwoods. Even on rainy days, they appeared in camp at unpredictable hours, raucously bugling for peanuts and trout skins. If Ringo was enjoying a bath in the lake or was sitting beside me on Speculation Log, those crow-sized gray-and-white pirates power-dived to pull fur from his coat before he could swat them away.

With goodies I encouraged their presence, because the flock trumpeted in concert whenever a daytime predator prowled. Whiskey-jacks followed us rather consistently wherever we went.

The rogue of Nicomen Lake did not qualify for membership in the Audubon Society. He was a bird lover all right, in the nasty sense that he sometimes sniffed out a covey of grouse chicks, raided all kinds of birds' nests, and five-fingered family collections of shiny nest ornaments. In these respects he qualified as a bird *watcher*. Where kingfishers, tanagers, or plovers pumped their wings or circled slowly above cattail reeds near the lakeshore, I knew that Ringo was bird-watching.

After a particularly delicious breakfast of late-summer bird eggs, Ringo bounced. Jumping up and down in one place is called the yo-yo complex. The raccoon yo-yoed with joy as he increased his collection of black feathers yanked from tails and wings during lakeside brawls with crows and ravens. He seemed to fight with large birds exclusively for the feathers he could pull out. He considered it an insult for me to interfere whenever he scrapped with any bird: duck, goose, grouse, raven, or ptarmigan. In pitched tantrums he also yo-yoed up and down like a paddled brat. When I panned him for robbing the nests of small birds, his sardonic smirk made it

70

plain that I should respect his God-given forage rights, regardless of what he foraged on. Twice when I lectured him—showing by the sound of my voice that I disapproved of overt acts of mischief that hurt another creature—he yo-yoed, did his fingernails, and preened his coat, unmistakable signs that he was ignoring me. He also bounded like a jumping jack when he wanted attention, food, or a shoulder ride. I do not mean to leave the impression that Ringo was insensitive to my approval. He valued my stamp of sanction perhaps more than anything else; he was often loathe to show it.

On September 4 an unusually vicious skirmish with ravens took place. Four birds included *me* in their grudge for my habit of taking Ringo's part when more than two ganged up on him. For my services in that fight, I received half a dozen scratches on my face and hands, a severely pecked nose, and a torn shirt. I could have wrung that pesky raccoon's neck for what I interpreted as an I-told-you-so look as he inspected my battered nose.

After the battle I followed the unwounded raccoon to the buckwheat and oat-grass heath above the lake's outlet. Given that he couldn't talk, I told myself that his obvious facial smirk existed only in my imagination because I had interfered.

The sunny hillside heath had ripened rich stands of seed-yielding grains. Ringo found most ripening seeds to his liking. Ancient glaciers had spread the base of the sloping meadow with flagstones. A species of ground

71

squirrel, called chickarees, had harvested and stored about a pound of dried mushrooms, as well as buckwheat and oat-grass seed, beneath each flagstone. Winter provender. As crafty and scheming as any fox you ever saw, tricky Ringo lifted one rock after another and feasted upon the chickaree's Hunger-Moon supplies. Outraged rodents shrilled from nearby shrubs and boulders. From the tone of certain chickaree voices and looks directed straight at me, I got the impression that they blamed me for allowing that scoundrel to plunder their winter stores.

During summer months when food is plentiful, Nicomen rodents store their dried berries, grain, and mushrooms in a variety of warehouses. They may not realize that other animals also observe their activities. Indian legend often refers to "Hunger Moons," the six months each year when starvation decimates entire communities—when predators become cannibals for lack of natural prey. Native Crees say that starvation during Hunger Moons is the Earth Mother's price for overpopulation.

That same Earth Mother neglected to invent padlocks for the stores of her wildlings. In high-altitude forests mammals that don't hibernate must hoard quantities of dried food that will not only outlast the Hunger Moons of late autumn and winter, but will also last until new growth is ripe enough to eat in April. Even after the Moon-of-Meltwater (March), the number-one killer of the northwoods is starvation.

His appetite for cereal grain satisfied for the moment, Ringo climbed to the top of a boulder, manicured his fingernails, and picked his teeth (all raccoons pick their teeth after eating foods that tend to catch between teeth). While practicing oral hygiene after his meal, he sat making mental notes as to where those furious and dull-witted rodents were hiding their remaining winter stockpiles—right in front of his larcenous eyes.

Contrary to popular belief, nature seldom escapes from making serious mistakes.

While Ringo primped, preened, and manicured away so many hours in early September, I worried up a storm. He may have been the only animal in the Nicomen basin refusing to put his house in order for winter. As a pot-bellied raccoon, he could sleep through perhaps two weeks of bad weather . . . provided, of course, he had a cold-proof den in which to snooze. At the end of two weeks, however, he would be obliged to wake up and go outside long enough to excrete and find a meal—a hefty meal! Two big kinks knotted his line: first, at that altitude every item of natural food would lie beneath twenty, maybe fifty, feet of snow; second, there were no cold-proof dens in the Nicomen basin. The rascal communicated the distinct impression that he had long ago entrusted such prosaic details to me. Presumably I had taken over his problems; therefore, normal major concerns no longer bugged him. There simply weren't enough hours in a day and night for the amount of fun we

73

were enjoying. In the meantime, he spent his wakeful moments clowning for all he was worth. I spent my time recording the things that were important to both of us as we lived them. To Ringo, coat and fingernails were more important than food and shelter; to me, a sunset, a fragrant meadow, a lone loon's song.

Shortly before noon on September 10, circumstances forced the raccoon to cope with a nerve-racking nuisance that refused to go away. Red squirrels barked, chattered, and spat without let-up. Their constant noise finally undercut Ringo's self-control. For once they succeeded in getting under his coat. He screamed with rage. There was only one escape. Down the beach.

With the gait and stride of a charging baboon, he rushed to my side, grabbed my pants leg, and begged to leave the noisy campsite before he started climbing imaginary walls. By then he had fought off the urge to be genuinely difficult even with me, so frazzled were his nerves. It was no easy task to keep up with him as he sped down the beach. Not even glancing toward his miniature cave, he raced into Nicomen Creek Canyon, surprisingly enough, toward the very spot where he had almost bumped noses with the lynx.

Less than sure of himself as we approached the boulder where the varmint had crouched, he shinnied up to my shoulder and straddled my neck. He knocked off my cap in order to cling to my hair, then purred like a kitten as he urged me down the canyon. Half a mile beyond the scene of our embarrassment I stopped to rest; he churred and trilled, clicked and clucked his tongue, gabbled and hissed until I resumed the journey. It was the first time he had objected when I wanted a second wind. I had no idea where he wanted to go. He did. So I went along.

Pleasant as it was to shuffle down the creekbank with a furry hitchhiker on my shoulders, it became necessary to make it less comfortable for him if I was to have strength enough left to reclimb that canyon on the way back to camp. For an example of his tyranny, he would cling to my Adam's apple with his feet, then use his hands to urge me to greater speed: yanked my hair, pulled my beard, twisted my ears. Worst of all, he thumped out a war dance on top of my head as if he were beating a tom-tom.

My progress through the brush improved when he decided that the bouncy ride on my shoulders, with branches slapping his face, afforded less comfort than walking on his own. Clutching my pants leg with one "hand," he urged me on down the canyon into dangerous-looking areas we had never explored together. Dank, smelly, and shivery in the half-light.

The farther down Nicomen Creek we rushed the denser grew the forest. Giant larch, hemlock, fir, and cedar competed both for sunlight and rootroom. Salal and vine-maple now locked arms with devil's-claw, firethorn, and gooseberry to form a stickery jungle on both banks. Progress was slowed to a laborious plod through squishy moss, stinky liverworts, and slimy fungi. Dozens

75

of fern-covered logs—some to climb over, others to go around—restricted much of our way. The canyon floor was dead and rotting, a weird landscape where death and rot appeared to be the same thing, and both stood fixed in solemn silence. Yeasty fingers of white mold death-gripped the trunks of standing, but long dead, trees. To spur me along, Ringo tugged at my jeans with one "hand" and pounded behind my knees with the other . . . in effect, a nuisance and a hindrance to the speed he seemed to want, to the irresistible feeling of emergency in his behavior.

At length we arrived where Nicomen Creek flowed into the Skaist River, more than two miles downstream from the outlet of Nicomen Lake. On the far (right) bank of the shallow Skaist, an ancient grove of balsam poplars—called cottonwoods in the United States—had crowded out the pines hundreds of years ago. At last the absence of overhead vines allowed sunlight to filter through the yellow autumn leaves. We crossed a solid mat of wire grass for about forty feet to reach the river's left bank and a slushy marsh. Gigantic poplars, by far the bulkiest trees I had ever seen in Canada, dominated the entire canyonscape. As we sloshed across the marsh, I saw that every exposed square foot of mud was stamped with *raccoon tracks*—all larger than Ringo's! His colony!

At last he had revealed his number-one secret.

Hackled to twice his normal size, my diminutive bandit now assumed a nervy lead like a prizefighter stepping into a ring to challenge an opponent. He began to chant

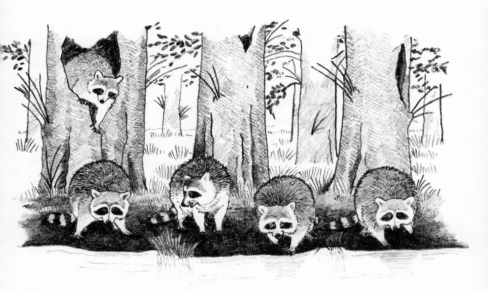

a loud, high-pitched battle cry in which I sensed the
makings of a brannigan. Having eased out of the hollow
cottonwood trunks without much pomp and ceremony,
five ominous *macho* raccoons swaggered to water's edge,
lined up, and swished their bushy, black-ringed tails.
Five ugly muzzles raised their lips and showed impres-
sive fangs. The big boars wigwagged their heads back
and forth like the shuttles of a loom. From outward expressions that shone on those five brutish mugs, Ringo
must have recognized the squint-eyed hatred of bad
blood. That mass of fangs, fists, and fortitude was vested
in bruisers far huskier than Ringo. With no intention of
giving quarter, they demanded immediate contest. Why
on earth, I asked myself, would that little fool of his own

free will take on *five* burly warriors at the same time, on their home soil, on their terms? They would skin him alive.

It never ceases to amaze visitors that Manning Provincial Park accommodates such extensive colonies of wild animals. One reason for the overpopulation is that relatively mild winters along the Similkameen River make food gathering no desperate problem for most species. But the main reason is that the region covers a borderland where several natural stomping grounds come together. Here one finds colonies of each species massed near the northern limits of native life zones. Raccoons and badgers, moose and timber wolves walk the same trails. Strangely, but true to natural logic, colonies of all species involved are scattered throughout the lower levels within Manning Park boundaries.

It may be safe to say that Ringo knew exactly where such boundaries existed and where numbers of his kind made their homes irrespective of man-made border lines. His approach to the cottonwood *coondominiums* suggested further evidence that he was *not* a human-raised animal. Pet raccoons panic at the very sight and smell of territory occupied by their wild cousins. The manifest hostility on the opposite bank of the Skaist indicated at the time that Ringo did not belong there under any circumstances. The five boorish *machos* stood ready to prove it.

7

The Outcast of Raccoonville

AFTER quickly appraising the muscle and fang power on the right bank of the Skaist, Ringo discreetly shed his feisty ambition to wage war. His high-pitched battle cry fizzled into a hummingbird whisper. Bristling hackles fell like wheat stalks in a tornado, while his side-to-side swagger dropped to a low belly-crawl. The pest of Nicomen Lake suddenly clambered hand over fist to my shoulders. He shuddered at the gates of Raccoonville as he had done when he faced the burl-batty bears and the long-legged lynx. His true character was thus exposed: he was a *paper tiger*.

Almost anyone could have guessed that most of Ringo's fears—real, imagined, and faked—came from the grief and anxiety of seven or eight weeks in exile. He was in reality a colony-type raccoon, expelled from his colony for some mysterious reason. Ruling bigwigs had banished him from his own kind where under normal circumstances he would have been preparing seriously for winter. Equipping cold-weather dens with linings in late August is a precaution northern raccoons observe with proper respect. By the time of his return to Raccoonville, his fickle wife would have chosen another partner to make ready their winter cuddling quarters. Ringo probably guessed his loss. Raccoons are polygamous, mating in January and February with hibernation companions.

Through signs and signals we had developed together, he indicated in no uncertain terms that I should take him back to Nicomen Lake posthaste.

Following our steep route up the canyon, we returned to the campsite no worse for the adventure. The next day we resumed our regular routines in the basin. Time and reality began to pass our low-profile life-style by. Regardless of daylight hour now, Nicomen skies were seldom without gossipy *V* after *V* as waterfowl plied the flyways en route to Mexican lagoons. Revealing no outward sign of hurry-scurry, doe wapiti and deer, nannies and ewes, and upland moose cows wandered past camp during the second week in September, leading their young down Heather Trail to lower elevations along the Similkameen and Skagit rivers where snow would not interfere seriously with ample winter pasture.

Warm southwesterly chinook winds from the Japanese Current reach Manning Park, walling off much of the winter cold that grips the interior of British Columbia. Nevertheless, the most alarming of several phenomena pointing toward early autumn arrived unexpectedly in the form of a northwesterly twister from the Gulf of Alaska. When polar gales defeated temperate chinooks, a freeze set in. Frost dropped every hardwood leaf and hayed the upland meadows. Fiery colors tinted sunset skies as autumn proclaimed itself across the face of our basin. I felt like an exile when the last yarrows, fireweeds, and goldenrods vanished from open hillsides, surrendering autumnal brilliance to winter gray-out.

Pondering the truths of heavy frost and the fact that my friend had indeed suffered banishment from Raccoonville, I formed a plan to relocate him in the sloughy backmarshes and shielding forests of the Similkameen Valley. As sober as a Pilgrim deacon, he sat on my lap and tried to read my thoughts.

The first really bad weather would prod me to put the plan in action. I loved the Nicomen Lake basin and would stay as long as possible with my friend. Little hope remained for Bigfoot clues unless extreme weather conditions forced a change in the creature's habitat.

By September 15, the full sweep of the Canadian Cascade Range basked in surprisingly gentle Indian summer. No wind, no rain, no frost. And only one attack on Ringo. A mother beaver gave him the paddling of his life for trying to force a wrestling match on her youngster. For a time at least the raccoon's food supply at the lake would hold out, provided, of course, he could keep a bevy of lurking predators from gnawing his bones. From the devil-may-care attitude that lit up his face, I doubted any possibility of peacemaking with his colony in the near future. My plan did not take such a reunion into account, but I didn't rule it out.

A raccoon expelled from a colony rarely reenters that same clan, because reentry precipitates a top-to-bottom reshifting within social ranks. Militant rule, called "swatting order," is profoundly important within a colony. The Alpha raccoon can swat any member of the settlement, but no raccoon dares swat Alpha. Beta can clobber anyone in the ranks except Alpha. Gamma can punch anyone except Alpha or Beta . . . and so on down the line to poor old Omega who pounds *no one*. Returning only pleasant grins, Omega must sit like a punching bag and absorb everyone else's wallops. "Pecking" or "swatting" order in most flocks, herds, and colonies has little to do with strength, size, age, or family status. Character virtues alone such as intelligence, personality, and leadership charisma limit a coon's social high-tide mark. A colony's most powerful young male may be *low man* on the totem pole; on the other hand, a mangy old female may rule from an Alpha or Beta post for years.

Several details made it unlikely that Ringo had commanded much rank in the Skaist River settlement. As his friend, I studied his complexes and hang-ups. He was a rebel, readily eager to challenge swatting order, thus overstepping his footing in the group. Any raccoon who stole more than he could carry would expose the group to retaliation. Overstealing, in other words, could have caused his banishment. His primping suggested a Don

82

Juan type who might just happen to serenade another stud's lawful wife. Eccentric behavior within a colony is taboo . . . for hermits only. Having spotted five boars each capable of outswatting him, I doubted that Ringo could have held a position of rank in that colony.

Although he trembled and wailed in the presence of danger, Ringo had lacked neither courage nor strength before my arrival at Nicomen Lake. Without such traits, he would not have survived his first week as an outcast. Therefore, I concluded that my influence upon him was increasingly bad . . . or that his make-believe "fear" may have demonstrated another facet of his fraud. With Ringo you couldn't be unmistakably sure about very much.

One detail, however, was almost beyond question. Instead of establishing himself either as a free-ranging agent with full ability to thrive alone, or as an Omega willing to absorb swats in some other colony, he used his superior intellect to achieve an alliance with a human being from whom he could leach food, shelter, and security. When I think how he conned me for sleeping space in the down bag! How he surrendered neither personal independence nor native clout by associating with man!

From his outward reactions I respected the fact that he sensed imaginary animals skulking about the underbrush looking for an opportunity to kill him. Of course, he could have staged those images also as an act to gain my sympathy and cinch his position in our alliance.

Crows, jays, marmots, martens, weasels, and some rodents that he met on his forage range would back down from their fierce-sounding bluff if he called their "hands" with a cranky growl or a slow, toothy charge of his own. Ravens continued to get his goat because they "played dirty pool," attacking him from the rear, outflanking him, and feinting false charges. He was justifiably wary of the very real creatures that stalked him wherever he went: Lynx, coyote, wolverine, and cougar would go to dangerous extremes in order to dine on raccoon drumsticks.

On September 18 Ringo had let down his guard to feast upon an unusual migration of short-horned grasshoppers along the shelflike meadows above Heather Trail. One such berm lay knee-deep in a tangle of weeds and grasses that small animals respected as hiding places for stalkers. The plant life had frosted into a mat of brown hay that locusts were ravaging.

Without warning and ignoring the human presence, Ringo's old enemy coyote sprang from behind a salt-and-pepper-colored boulder and pounced upon the screaming raccoon. For a moment I fought off a spontaneous impulse to interfere. I waved the alpenstock. At that moment the raccoon probably thought I had gone chicken.

Then all reason for human meddling disappeared. During the rolling struggle that followed, Ringo's vice-like jaws and needle-sharp teeth clamped around the coyote's windpipe. The raccoon demonstrated the survival value of his four "hands" with sixteen "fingers" and four "thumbs" by shredding the coyote's lips. Within a minute, however, he released his death grip on the song-dog's throat and ran to my feet without killing the enemy that had harried him on several occasions. Had my taming influence changed the raccoon's hereditary ways, causing him to forego natural killer instinct in a life-and-death battle? I don't know. The bleeding coyote yelped and howled down the trail, probably never to return to the Nicomen basin.

Besides coyotes and big cats, one other enemy gave cause for worry: the wolverine. These dangerous killers are often called carcajous or gluttons by northwoodsmen. Twice from a respectful distance we had glimpses of this reddish-brown, slow-moving cousin of fishers, otters, weasels, and skunks. Not until September 20, however, did the evil-tempered hermit show his true colors. From his skin-and-bones appearance, the carcajou seemed more than half-starved. On the early morning of that day, Ringo worked up the nerve to lead me to the wolverine's den, hoping no doubt that I would dispatch this dangerous enemy. As we neared the deep-forest lair—a burrow under two fallen hemlocks—the enraged predator rushed out, growled like a bear, and exhibited his terrible, toothy grimace. He sprayed the opening of his den with foul-smelling musk, somewhat milder than skunk "squeezin's" but bad enough. I was delighted when he retreated into the forest high above Ringo's own den at the outlet of the lake. Why the mustelid had not eaten the raccoon long before will have to remain one of those unanswered questions of northland mystique. Ringo and I recognized the animal's simulated "cowardice" as a clever trick. Knowing that there are no cowards among wolverines, we never once let him out of our sight. And a good thing we didn't.

To me the most astonishing discovery was the fact that wolverines are perhaps the most outlandish thieves in Canada. This one at Nicomen Lake had stacked inside and about his den five dozen large and heavy articles of no possible use to him. Weighing about ten pounds more than Ringo, the pirate had scrounged a cast-iron skillet (one-sixth his own weight), a shovel, several axes, hatchets, a single-jack sledgehammer, an automobile jack, numerous large wrenches, a gasoline lantern, rods, reels, pots, assorted cans, and a camper's portable "potty"—to name but a few. Clearly he had hooked most of his loot from the public campground in the Similkameen Valley. Between his jaws he had carried at least half a ton of metal gear for a distance of more than *seven miles* over rough, steep, uphill trail.

The ill-tempered glutton, slowly circling and appraising us, launched a direct charge within five minutes. In close quarters at the opening of the reeking den, it was impossible to know whether Ringo or I would bear the brunt of the carcajou's first slashing attack. The raccoon decided not to stick around long enough to find out. I

was close on his heels. When my friend headed toward the lake, the wolverine cut him off. The ugly predator stood on his hind legs like a bear and swung his most effective swat. The blow caught Ringo low on the rump, lifted him off the ground, and sent him hurtling ten feet through the air. The amazing swat was even more remarkable when you consider one single fact: the wolverine weighed at most ten pounds more than the raccoon . . . rather conclusive verification that the carcajou is indeed the strongest mammal on earth—pound for pound.

Growling like a guard dog, Ringo recovered his footing. He was madder than a pinched hornet. We did not wait for the wolverine's second attack, which was aimed at me. At the same instant Ringo's sharp teeth and my alpenstock contacted the brute's hind quarters with surprising shock effect, if not damage. At any rate, the mauler raced up the nearest tamarack to reconnoiter. While still in one piece, my friend and I hightailed it for open beach, but not before I had "borrowed" his best looking ax. We knew what to expect if we hung around and waited for the glutton to slide down that lodgepole. Except for his foul odor and hot breath close to my head at the pup tent's mosquito flap at night, he seldom revealed himself so openly again during the rest of my stay in the basin. Nor did he ever try to reclaim his ax.

Recovering somewhat from the shocking wolverine experience, we spent most of September 21 and 22 inside the shelter. Actually we caught up on sleep—and I brought my notes up to date—because of steady rain that fell for two days without let-up. Between lengthy snoozes, I organized my log with the idea of sharing Nicomen Lake adventures with other raccoon fans. Since every second thought concerned Ringo's resettlement, I studied government topo maps of the Similkameen region with the object of finding a suitable habitat in which to relocate him. After studying details of the map, I found nothing to my liking.

On the twenty-third an east wind swept the sky free of rain clouds. Warm Indian summer returned. According to the map, a small bench lake called Iceberg lay in a narrow trough (bench) high above timberline beyond where the bears had grazed. Surrounded by knify ridges and located about three miles above camp, the lake had no visible outlet, no visible source—other than seepage. I had never been to Iceberg Lake—even during ambitious jaunts for evidence of Bigfoot.

When Ringo saw me bearproof the rucksack and take up the alpenstock, he danced to his single, softly mumbled "tune." Rushing to the beach, he finger-sketched strange outlines in the wet sand. I suddenly remembered that he had made similar "drawings" earlier. I had copied his "art work" in my notebook, hoping he would repeat even *one* of the characters he "drew." He never did. Apparently the only meaning he put into the sketches was an expression of wild joy anticipating the next adventure. He may have been trying to reproduce some of the many outlines he had seen me draw in my notebook. Raccoons are notorious copycats.

The hike to that distant lake wore Ringo out. I fared little better. The difference was that he plunged into the lake for refreshment. I put one finger into the icy water and thought for sure I would suffer hypothermia. During our walk around the sapphire-blue Iceberg Lake, we found not so much as one mouthful of anything that either of us could eat.

For the sake of adventure, I decided upon a different cross-country route back to Nicomen Lake. We had gone less than a hundred yards when a rustle of falling gravel behind us jolted our attention toward an ugly terrorist that had been stalking us all morning. That horrid wolverine had carefully accomplished the impossible: Heaven only knows what kind of backstabbing the mugger had planned had he not slipped on that gravel. A strange enough sight, the brute stood on his front paws, sprayed skunklike musk into the air, then fled like a scared rabbit.

There were other terrorists to assault us when we returned to Nicomen Lake. Because of what prowled near camp during the next several days, I almost wished either to leave the vicinity or arm myself with a high-powered rifle. I knew I could never use a rifle.

8

The Pinch of Hunger

SEVERAL deadly encounters with big predators proved
that Ringo was no full-blooded coward, even though fear
often needled him. In his brawl with the coyote, he had
declined to kill, yet he learned the necessity for giving a
first-class account of himself when bullies attacked. Loss
of his position in the colony may have discouraged his
will to fight back until the wolverine and the coyote
forced him to stand his ground. His self-defense proved
to be better ecology than his love for mischief. Unless
mischief and larceny were means of shoring up his self-
image, they served precious little purpose toward survival. His natural disposition toward plain bad behavior,
however, would still breed scabs for his nose.

Strong hints of escalating danger kept us both on the
alert. We read it in one another's eyes: a warning concerning those moving shadows that increased in number
and padded closer each night along the edge of the forest
behind the campsite and tent while we sat and speculated on Speculation Log near a campfire that no enemy

dared approach. When fear tormented Ringo, he panted as if he had just climbed Nicomen Ridge. My own reaction was to turn clammy cold. It was not unreasonable to believe that Ringo's dream-ridden sleep and mental terror probably invented images of beasts that could not possibly exist.

An imaginary threat often frightens more than the real thing. We fear most what we do not understand. The grizzly bear without question has proven itself the bravest animal on earth, but an adult grizzly dares not climb a tree for *fear* of falling. I once saw a pika stampede a herd of bighorn sheep.

Two of Ringo's more earthly "ghosts" appeared on the twenty-fourth. We were walking down the beach at the beginning of our morning browse. In order to deceive enemies whose hunting success depended most upon fixed habits of their prey, we rarely followed the same forage route two days in succession. Abruptly the raccoon broke into a lope for about sixty feet.

Without a moment's warning (as was always the case), two coyotes rushed from a willow thicket and charged the masked bandit in two different circular patterns of attack similar to strategy used by the foxes after the burglary of their lair. Honoring my resolution to train him back to the wild, I offered no immediate help. He may have sensed that I had quietly rushed to the scene in order to stand prepared to exercise the well-seasoned manzanita walkingstick should the two predators seriously threaten his life. Like a bear, he stood erect on his hind legs but shouted no appeal for help. Both coyotes turned down his invitation to embrace. They may have known that he could cut a jugular vein in a fiftieth of a second.

Proving his ability to think clearly in a crisis (or act through instinct, if you prefer), the nimble-witted Ringo plunged into the lake the moment he saw himself the target of a meat-eater on each side. Through smell memory he probably recognized his attackers as the same dark forms that prowled while we sat and shuddered on Speculation Log. Although it embarrasses me to confess it, we both did much more shuddering than speculating on that Log!

At any rate, the raccoon swam with admirable speed into water that was at least six feet deep, then dog-

paddled around to face his enemies. At that time he weighed roughly thirty-eight pounds, perhaps six or seven pounds less than a coyote. Under water he could hold his breath a full minute longer than *any* coyote, a condition known among betting men as the "edge of leverage." No *fifty*-pound animal other than a wolverine could support a thirty-eight-pound raccoon around his neck, especially if the raccoon cinched his jaws around the attacker's windpipe and put his destructive hands to work ripping flesh. In fact, had the coyotes pursued Ringo into deep water, he could have drowned them both with little extra effort, provided his killer instinct survived. Respecting the raccoon's capability ahead of time, the two hungry song-dogs yodeled a few dry notes, then disappeared into the forest under my hail of egg-sized stones.

But the days of empty bellies were not far distant, when predators would learn to plan their attacks with greater accuracy or starve. Hunger would force them to catch a raccoon before he could jump into the water. And worst of all—most predators must have known that the lake would soon freeze over!

Upland birds, many mammals, and most flying insects had left the Nicomen watershed by September 25. At that date fear of hunger and memory of empty guts were still more terrible than present hunger itself. Scarcity of available prey turned normal creatures into wastrels. What remained of the rapidly failing food supply caused greedy appetites to commit excesses before Hunger Moons began in mid-November. Rather than follow migrating prey—as northern timber wolves do—local predators hunted night and day, slaughtering more rodents, hares, and young of remaining hoofed mammals than they could possibly eat. Although lasting for a few days only, this practice resulted in temporary good fortune for Ringo. He fought with smaller competitors in order to muscle in on trailside feasts. Time and again I shagged after him as he followed his nose or a flight of ravens to carcasses that had barely begun to decay. No animal, regardless of size, interfered while the wolverine ate. Coyotes and foxes stayed out of swatting range when cougar and lynx feasted. Every creature in the basin except the wolverine respected the mother skunk's mealtime. Depending upon my proximity with a stick, Ringo challenged many small diners. He and Pewberty often competed for the biggest mouthfuls but never squabbled over quarry.

Late September dawns, cold and dangerous, became as silent as sunsets. Ringo and I strained to catch single notes at a time of day that in summer had bubbled with songs from every quarter. Thin, chilly atmosphere carried sounds farther than summer air—when there were sounds to carry.

At sunrise on the twenty-sixth I sat like a bronc-buster with my heels gouged into Speculation Log. Struggling to get my share from a pot of sweetened cornmeal mush and canned milk, I repented the mistake of allowing Ringo to eat from the same utensil. Except for trailside carrion, his food supply had become a serious problem, so I supplemented it now and then to keep him from losing the vital prehibernation fat he had accumulated.

During those breakfasts there was no escape from him. I could stand up and walk away with a pot of food only to have him climb to my shoulders and help himself anyway. You could not stretch an arm where he couldn't go. My only chance lay in native ability to chew and swallow faster than a raccoon.

The hot mush scuffle at last concluded, we sat staring at each other on the Log near the fire pit. An ever-so-slight rustle on forest duff required attention—a reflex action to any silent-dawn noise not our own. Suddenly Ringo leaped to my shoulders, trilled like a steam loco-motive, and pounded the top of my head (a habit of his in moments of crisis). I stood and gawked with astonish-ment at a nervy pine marten slightly larger than a do-mestic cat. The strikingly colorful sable raced about camp, emitting squeaks and smelly musk. My Okanagan Cree cousins predict early snow whenever this ex-tremely shy animal climbs down from treetops and visits a human being. That particular marten in an exquisite reddish-brown coat ignored the hissing fussbudget on my shoulders and accepted salted nuts from my hand—an unusual change from his normal diet of birds, squir-rels, and insects—possibly a yearning for salt. Ringo behaved toward our polite guest like the prince of imps that he was. He shouted and hissed a steady flow of huff at me for feeding the marten. He hung onto my jacket collar with his hind "hands," waved his arms, and continued to swat me about the head while shrieking and whistling at the sable.

After less than five minutes, the gentlemanly marten had endured more than his fill of that noisy raccoon. He tripped away with speed and grace, disappearing into deep forest shadows. His brisk exit may have been triggered by the whistle of a rising norther that soon extinguished any further hope of sunrise tranquility and surprises that day.

After the marten's brief visit and before we began to face the norther along spent forage trails, Ringo sat and studied my eyes. At last quiet, he rocked back and forth on Speculation Log. Before leaving camp, we waited for the sun to burn off a web of sharp frost needles that bristled like cactus thorns across the bottom of every low place throughout the basin. There was something on that coon's mind.

Because Ringo's world had become a gauntlet of fangs and claws, I was a bit disappointed that he had not jumped from my shoulders and challenged the marten the moment the well-behaved little gent entered camp. Staying alive in that eat-or-be-eaten wilderness would seem to demand more than the shake of a fist or the utterance of abusive squawks when another mammal barged in to share the wealth. In a truly wild state he

would have launched physical force against any car-
nivore he could have whipped. For his own good, I
wanted to see him win a few fights.

According to plan, the day of the marten was our day
to forage the marsh one mile north of camp in the canyon
below the lake's outlet. We had faced the knify gale for
little more than halfway when long-faced Ringo communicated in no wishy-washy terms that we were about to
share a new kind of terror.

In the same hideous flash we both glimpsed a huge,
ghostly, black monster that had exposed himself for a
fraction of a second while slipping from the lakefront into
the dusky forest behind us. Although hidden in thick
stands of shrubs and trees, the fiend was not only stalking Ringo and me, he was running like an Olympic
sprinter. Making no effort to soft-pedal his crash through
forest underbrush, he headed our way at a dreadful clip,
an upright runner!

My mind suddenly overflowed with gruesome Indian
tales of Hunger Moons . . . and *a hungry Sasquatch!* My
nerve vanished. Weeks had passed since I had lost hope
of Bigfoot evidence, and there it was, chasing me down
the basin. Charging at reckless speed through the sticks
inside the forest, the ape-man was coming from the direction of our camp. He had no doubt wrecked my
equipment, shredded the sleeping bag and tent, and
gulped what little grub I had left. But that wasn't the
worst. The monster was rapidly subtracting the distance
between us.

From the beginning of my project, I had rehearsed various means of escape should the giant hominid appear. I had pictured myself calmly rocking back and forth on Speculation Log, planning to smile and offer the king-sized monkey a handful of peanuts. Should my charity prove unacceptable, I could count on natural fear to propel me down Heather Trail faster than any Sasquatch could run—hopefully. I had even pictured myself as the hero of the day: staring the brute down, demanding that he follow me to park headquarters and turn himself in. How the dickens did I assume the gorilla understood English?

On that frightful morning I forgot all plans for escape. I must admit that planned routines of any kind were an abomination neither of us would have respected. But what could I do to save Ringo? An idea popped into my confused head: run as fast as possible with my ward to Raccoonville near the Skaist River. The husky inhabitants might lend their muscle; ten or twelve boar coons could stir up a monumental scrap. Surely Sasquatch wouldn't risk his winter coat to such a chewing and tearing.

So, without even a backward glance toward the rackety crashing in the forest, I seized my trembling companion by the tail, threw him over one shoulder like a sack of potatoes, and cut out for the canyon as if jet-propelled.

9

The Bigfoot Scare

RINGO hated to be lifted by the tail, but during that emergency he neither fussed nor tried to free himself. He clung to my jacket with all four "hands." Anything to get lost at that point. Expecting the worst when I realized that I could never outrun Sasquatch down that thorny, slushy canyon, I dived into the wreckage of an old-time trapper's cabin in the trees above the beach.

Ringo received unmistakable communication that I would choke him if he so much as breathed. Because of caved-in walls and no windows, we were unable to see our pursuer. Backpackers had sometimes reported grizzly bears at Nicomen Lake. If our Sasquatch turned out to be a grizzly, we could climb a tree and be safe; but being an ape, Bigfoot was probably born to trees.

My boss in Southern California believed that the Nicomen basin was the capital of Sasquatchia.

When I stuck my head out for a quick and careful peek, our position went sour without prospect of escape. The creature had seen our hiding place.

Like a condemned man receiving a reprieve, I took a second look, because I didn't believe the first. Loping down the beach and bolting straight for the caved-in cabin, raced a yearling black bear. Disbelieving my eyes, I looked around for Sasquatch. Only a bear. My breathing resumed just as my color changed from dark purple. Ringo, who still crouched in my lap with his arms around my waist, clung to two belt loops and whined. I interpreted his squeak as, "What the devil do you see?" As we climbed from the tumbled-down shack, sheepish grins crept over our faces. Ringo sputtered like a faulty package of firecrackers, while I spoke some shameful words I would not repeat.

The bear, between one and two years old, proved to be a humble and friendly little female whose life-style was that of a vagabond, panhandling around Manning Park. I had never seen her before. She looked more than half-starved. Most abandoned yearling bears are. By then a professional freeloader, she was no doubt used to associating with people, a regular caller at Hampton Campground in the Similkameen River valley where bears regularly mooch handouts. By the end of September most campers were long gone, but a few diehard fishermen remained. From possibly seven or eight miles she had sniffed our campfire and the smells of food. All she had to do was follow Heather Trail. I wondered if that bear was what Ringo had on his mind before we left camp. Had he smelled her approach?

Anyway, there she stood on her hind paws, waltzing

101

around like a trained gypsy performer, "singing" the old gutbucket tune—an act perfected to guarantee payoff by sympathetic campers.

"Come on, Ringo," I said. "We'll have to fix her a bite to eat. She's starving."

Then, like a bolt of lightning, the most startling observation of my entire stay in the Nicomen basin suddenly struck me. On the way back to camp my legs almost buckled at the sight: The way a legend gets started can be indeed simple. And what could be simpler than a yearling's footprints in the moist sand? When she galloped, her left hind paw stepped on the rear half of the track that the left forepaw had imprinted. She stamped the same impression on the right side. Because of her bowlegged forearms, she printed spoor that would convince the most skeptical to believe that Sasquatch himself had lumbered across the damp ground. The bear and the raccoon had to run in order to keep up with me on the way back to camp. Strangely, Ringo showed no hint of fear of the yearling; she showed no resentment of him. They became instant friends. From his behavior and that familiar look in his eyes, I suspected that he might possibly have some hanky-panky up his "sleeve"—at least a practical joke or two with which to entrap our new playmate.

With a deaf ear turned toward the howling monkey on my shoulder, I dipped into a dwindling food supply and fed the yearling until her belly was as tight as a drumhead. Sensible people would have condemned such irresponsibility even had I been flush on grub. Man's unnatural and processed foods break a bear's native eating habits with incurable damage to digestive organs. Perhaps worse yet, handouts of human goodies alter a wild animal's instinct to remain independent. I knew all of that, but she was *so* hungry . . . and I was *so* happy she had turned out to be a bear!

After her brief meal I went back to the beach, sprayed a pair of footprints in order to preserve every detail, then poured plaster of Paris into the deceptive impressions in the sand. While the castings hardened, the bear and the raccoon got better acquainted by roughhousing up and down the beach—to the extent that they destroyed all but two remaining prints—fortunately a left and a right. Only when loping, did she make the apelike prints. With the prospect of an amiable four-legged companion, Ringo went crazier than a monkey in a banana market.

Four plaster moulages turned out to be as nearly flawless as anyone could want. Later on they were destined to cast doubts more upon me than upon the romantic Bigfoot fable. Imagine my misguided daydream that this new evidence might withdraw the charming myth permanently from circulation! Little did I ever suspect that they would come near to landing me in the slammer.

The rogue of Nicomen basin soon regarded the bear as his second defender. That very morning he learned for a fact that the yearling posed no serious threat even when he badgered her patience. The worst she did was hiss

103

when with angelic expression the coon pulled her matted fur, chewed stubby black claws, pinched soft underbelly, and crammed exploring fingers into her mittlike ears. During those very busy first hours while he explored her "from stem to stern," the impudent little demon took me apart with his eyes. I got his message all right. He learned quickly enough how much I would take before walloping his rear end, and he wanted to know for sure just how far he could go with the bear. He accepted her light clobbering and learned to roll like a bowling ball when he earned a real sidewinder to the fanny.

Despite loud objections, one afternoon she caught him and held him down for a vigorous spit bath. Bears love to bathe cubs; to her, Ringo was a cub. From her jumbled mumblings and cooings, one could have thought she was experiencing the mother-bear instinct. My refusal to help Ringo when she pinned him down inspired the brat to take out his revenge in the sleeping bag where he spit-bathed my naked back until midnight.

By and large the yearling's simplicity and gentle manners provided the frisky raccoon with a harmless and much-needed punching bag. She doted upon no arbutus burl but did pledge allegiance to one selected fir tree, which she embraced, licked, clawed, chewed, and inspected frequently. She placed sticks and pinecones near the trunk of her "shrine," presumably as ornaments or gifts. Each day she sprinkled the trunk generously with urine to let all wildlife know that the tree was hers. If Ringo so much as went near the sanctuary—which he often did when he found out that it pestered her—the bear hissed like saliva on a hot stove. I believe he recognized potential dynamite in her clumsy wallop. He learned quickly to gauge her range.

Because of sluggish imagination, the bear also allowed incorrigible little Ringo to find out that she hated the cold, icy stare. He absorbed some hefty swats by deliberately gawking at her with a deadpan "grin" that she hated. I was not completely convinced that Ringo was not experimenting with the strange language of eyes that sometimes bridges a gulf between species. The bear put up with almost every kind of devilment from that renegade, but she refused to tolerate deliberate, empty gapes. Nine times out of ten it was her *threatened* swat that put him in line. Being *considered* dangerous carries real clout and survival advantages in the boonies.

Almost at once the yearling and I began to communicate in ways that rarely required words or other physical expression. We conveyed many meanings through eyes and limited gestures. Only slightly less than a speaking animal by nature, she learned my optical signals within a week. It took longer for me to learn hers.

Hungry or stuffed, the bear acted like a child who had missed the fun part of growing up. Her first few days with two incurable fun lovers must have required embarrassing, if not confusing, adjustments. At first she did not know when we were serious or playing. Finally, she and Ringo chose me for endless indignities: maulings, bitings, slaps, clawings, and general abuse. They somehow got the idea that my arms and legs existed solely for chewing purposes or for sharpening claws. The two even tried to root me out of my own tent! Still and all, they were superb companions in one of the most magnificent of the last unspoiled wildernesses on the North American continent.

For her safety under deep boondocks conditions, I taught her to respond to the name *Wahnoma,* a Cree word meaning "woman bear." For the sake of convenience, I shortened it to plain *Noma.* An animal regards a name given by a human being as a vocal signal that demands a response—nothing more than a call to attention. Voice tone, eyes, and gestures communicate most to a bear or a raccoon. Repetition is the key.

106

Ringo learned to respond to the call of his name within a day. He cringed when I shouted, *"Ringo!"* in disapproval of certain kinds of mischief. I hated the role of disciplinarian.

Bears learn much faster than dogs and remember longer, according to my experience. Noma learned, for instance, that she was among the most vulnerable of forest creatures. The fact that she had no mother must have caused her inordinate suffering during those first months on her own. She rushed to every animal she met, probably to discover that no one ever wanted her. The cranky-eyed wolverine invited her to his den, but Ringo must have communicated. Sensitive to alarm, she quickly linked the carcajou's musk with danger. A forty-five-pound wolverine can easily kill a bear weighing 250 pounds.

Fortunately for Wahnoma, the two local bear families had already toted their arbutus burl to the Pasayten River country across the international border in the state of Washington. They would have clobbered the orphan.

So, she stayed with us and responded as if we were the first two completely friendly beings she had known in her short lifetime. She even learned to play . . . and thus I was mauled. But I loved every minute of it.

Yet, shrinking food sources now seriously threatened every permanent resident the length and breadth of the Cascades. Each day saw another large mammal round up his family and head for more flourishing territory—the river valleys. During our forage walk on the last day of September, Noma and Ringo worked hard for two hours without tasting one bite of food. For a fleeting moment I entertained the notion of leading both animals from the basin to a more clement biome below. The idea was only a toy: a dream to establish both bear and raccoon in a gentler land for their sakes.

On the night of the thirtieth we underwent a cloudburst. Noma foraged alone into the night, but Ringo and I squirmed into the dry pup tent. We had been asleep for perhaps two hours when the bear barged into camp to join us. Her wet fur dripped puddles and stank like decaying flesh. Her paws were gummy with mud. Her breath reeked of wild onions and carrion maggots. Until that night she had slept near the mosquito netting *outside* the pup tent. There was no possible space for her inside that one-man shelter, even had I consented to stench and mess. But she did not understand. She scratched, pawed, and puffed her withering breath inside.

Then, the moment I crawled outside to restrain her attack on the tent, she dashed inside. She had misunderstood my signals. There was nothing for me to do but tie a nylon tarp between two trees and sit up for the rest of a miserable night. Soaking wet, I almost froze while Ringo and Noma snored inside the luxury of a waterproof tent, on an expensive, down-filled sleeping bag. The two bogtrotters turned my neat bedroom into a disaster area.

That sleepless night, however, did give me time to reach a decision: to goad both animals down Heather Trail to the Similkameen Valley.

108

Rain stopped at daybreak on October 1. After an extravagant breakfast—almost enough for the three of us—I packed my wet and muddy gear and coaxed both objecting friends to follow me down the trail. While I worried about their immediate future, those two clowns turned the trip into a circus act. They boxed, rolled, chased, and complained about having to leave the territory they enjoyed: that barren, starving Nicomen basin.

Resembling anything but a trail, the oozy route soon plunged into dense forest. A few sullen clouds from the rainstorm still sulked around the shoulders of the Brothers Peaks. Wind wheezed through the pines as if it had the sniffles. At length we detoured around a small marsh because a pair of incredibly arrogant moose believed they owned the entire park. They threatened to prove it.

Finally we left the drippy forest. Then shortly after

noon we arrived at Hampton Public Campground on the left bank of the Similkameen River. The worst thing happened when a camper's two poodles attacked Noma and Ringo. From then on, everything went counterclockwise. No sooner had the yelling owner grabbed his two wounded mutts than Wahnoma seized half a ham from a camp table, sped away, and gulped huge bites when she stopped out of rock-throwing range. At the same time Ringo unraveled another camper's plate of spaghetti. There were very few campers at that time of the year, but one had to be a CB-radio buff.

Answering the man's SOS, a Royal Canadian Mounted Police patrol, in full-dress, bright-red and striking-blue uniforms, sirened a royal parade into the campground in a rattly old Ford pickup. Their first official act was to declare both animals dangerous nuisances. I was declared a *simple* nuisance, probably not dangerous.

Both Noma and Ringo were condemned to death and sentenced to be shot immediately!

10

The Wind Also Scolded

CAMPERS still bellowed about Noma and Ringo, but they roared even louder at the Mounties for handing down death sentences. With both animals now tugging on leashes—the ham paid for—the spaghetti and punished poodles apologized for—I appealed to the RCMP with the gold braid on his uniform.

"I plan to release both animals in the lower Similkameen Valley about twelve miles below here," I said. Ringo shinnied to my shoulders and sat as erect as an MP at the Queen's picnic. He clacked his fingernails, hissed like a whistling teakettle, poked out his tongue, and showered the handsome officer with lowly coon spit. Wahnoma stood on her hind paws and slapped back and forth at me and the lead encircling her neck. I was surprised that both animals tolerated their leashes.

A scowling young Okanagan park attendant approached. He stopped within eavesdropping distance, leaned against a tree, fired up his pipe, then silently memorized the scene. His long, black braids dangled from beneath a wide-brimmed, once-white Stetson. His eyes were steel-gray and cold, his scowl severe enough for that of a witch doctor invoking a haunting. Somehow I sensed an ally, but he made no effort to come to my rescue.

The uniformed dudes jawed for a moment in official *ecologicaldegook*, then shot down my plan.

"That region's already overcrowded with winter migrants, Leslie," said the gold-braided officer. I detected a hint of leniency in his tone, now that a dozen campers stood by and mumbled.

"Scarcity o' native pickin's, you know," said his subordinate. "Both bear and raccoon would soon get ripped by permanent resident animals. They'd start raidin' farmers downstream and get wasted for sure. Then we'd catch Old Nick for lettin' 'em go."

"So, forget it," said the man in command. "Drag 'em back where you got 'em or we'll shoot 'em!"

The good-looking Okanagan puffed at his pipe and took me apart with a series of X-ray glances. His expression revealed something that troubled him. His penetrating look definitely carried a message—as an animal's eyes would—about those two wiggly brats on leash. But I failed to read the Indian. The poodle man insinuated something about Yanks that become infatuated with bears and raccoons. With absurd looks of innocence characteristic of neither, Ringo and Noma jabbered a blue streak. Without ceremony, except that of the raccoon dancing on my shoulders and pounding

112

the top of my head as usual (to the howling delight of several campers), we began the long slog back up the highway to that rugged forest route to Nicomen Lake.

Both Redcoats and the scowling Indian stared fixedly at us until we were out of sight on Heather Trail. At least we were all alive! Without a monitoring conscience to flog them, the two outcasts cavorted all the way back to the basin.

But the winds of October continued to scold, to inflict dismal changes in the high country. Coyotes badgered Ringo even before we left camp for forage the next morning. Noma rushed from her bear-tree rituals in order to prevent the howl-dogs from cutting off the raccoon's escape into the lake. A pair of hard-pressed fishers heckled him on the beach, then slashed at the bear. The predators took cover when Noma stood on her hind paws and started throwing right and left uppercuts. Her thick fur, like Ringo's rich, downy winter underwear, protected her from sharp, fast teeth. I raced to the scene with the alpenstock when the shadow of a cougar flashed between two gooseberry shrubs. Forest half-light failed to hide one sleazy wolverine that stalked our camp most of the time. We had known predators, yes, but no such numbers had prowled day and night about the campsite before we got the bum's rush from Hampton Campground.

Ringo's skunk friend Pewberty assumed a hostile attitude toward Noma. With his tail above the firing port, he threatened with clout that even the most uninitiated bear could understand instinctively. Skunks don't arbitrate; they *precipitate*—with a concealed weapon. Even Mrs. Mephitis and her five Xerox-copy kits—all friends of Ringo—refused en masse to accept Wahnoma. The bear simply ignored skunk snubs and went about her business.

When at last I found a little time for sunset inspiration alone on Speculation Log, I recoiled at the naked truth that October's freezing gales would soon force me to leave whether I wanted to or not. Snow could hide the trail to the bus stop near Manning Park HQ. As more frigid wind chided, my complicated dilemma produced less inspiration.

Before retiring, I made Noma understand that she was not to enter that pup tent again. Apparently she understood when I shook the alpenstock at her, because she never tried to root me out after that.

Having planned originally to leave by September, I had brought no snowshoes, no woolen long johns, no parka, no cold-weather food. Marmots and ground squirrels had already burrowed below the frost line to sleep out the jeering winds of winter. Fat pikas sat near their garnered haystacks and whistled during icy northers . . . their voices seemed to yell, "Beat it! Beat it!"

Within a nick of giving up hope, I decided on October 4 to expose Ringo once more to Raccoonville. Maybe they would allow him a small nook in which to winter. To my surprise, he followed eagerly down the brushy can-

114

yon, almost as if to confirm my suspicions that a native internal motivation of some kind goaded him to take high-risk chances. We left Wahnoma pottering around the marsh. She chased shadows to satisfy mental hunger, dug cattail tubers to silence rumbling intestines.

When Ringo and I reached the gaunt and leafless cottonwood grove, that same reception committee-of-five bare-toothed *machos* with raised hackles paced the right bank and dared us to cross the Skaist, a stream not more than three inches deep at that time of the year. While Ringo hissed, growled, and bared his own teeth from my shoulders, I splashed across to the right bank to undertake a problem I didn't even understand. Unwilling to oppose a man with a big stick, the sentinels growled for a moment before plunging headlong into hollow cottonwoods. They all hummed in unison like high-tension power lines. When I tried to shove Ringo into the first opening, he squirmed and fluttered as if I were exposing him to certain death. He trembled, shrieked, and clawed to get away. Then he turned, looked me in the eye, ground his teeth, and dove into the cavern inside the trunk.

The battle that followed in those confined quarters shook the giant shell of the tree. For fifteen minutes muffled snarls, squeals, thumps, and grunts spouted through the several openings: great knot holes that led from the interior literally steamed like chimneys on that frosty morning. At last an air of tranquillity hovered about the grove. Several masked faces poked from port-

115

holes in a neighboring cottonwood, as if awaiting a news bulletin from the scene of battle. I accused myself of having forced a trusting friend to an untimely, horrible death.

High overhead the helmeted face of a barred owl peeped over a battlement opening of the combat tree. Suddenly the owl received a rude shove from behind, forcing the bird to the wing. Ringo's angry face appeared on the parapet. He remained for a moment only, like a bear cub sitting on a bumblebee.

But he was injured. Gobs of fur had been torn from his coat. Blood dripped from slashes about his head and shoulders. Unable to lick his wounds on the precarious outer edge ramparts, he crawled through the opening and climbed down the outside to the tree's fork. He stopped there and focused an enigmatic gaze on my face . . . it may have been an "urge-to-kill" gaze.

A brooding mystery of stillness lingered inside the *coondominium*. At length Ringo backed all the way down the bark of the cracked and knotty trunk. I lugged him across the river on my shoulders, while an audience looked on from the cottonwoods and hissed. Then I dunked Ringo in the river in order to cool his wounds and wash away the blood. To compound my shame at that unhappy moment, there stood Noma, in all probability assuming that I was trying to drown Ringo for some reason. When the raccoon saw the bear, the scandalous rogue made my deed look like the real thing. Under the dark visor of his face mask, his eyes swiveled as if he were partly conscious. His angelic disguise masked a barbarous heart itching for revenge. Fortunately, by then I think Noma knew the tricky little varmint as well as I did, maybe better.

Even though we allowed the raccoon to set the pace, our upstream hike back to Nicomen Lake was cold, slow, and painful. Ringo snarled and spat whenever I tried to carry him, but he never threatened to bite. Each time the agony of his cuts and bruises became unbearable, he staggered to the creek and sat in deep pools where he submerged his head to cool his wounds. At camp he shook himself dry by the campfire, then crept into the pup tent without even asking to share supper. Noma, as noiseless as an owl, circled the campsite a few times but refused to approach Speculation Log, by all appearances convinced that I had indeed whaled the daylights out of Ringo.

On the day he received the bloody head and shoulders, Ringo had proved to himself that he could defy swatting order or "peck rights" and fight even when outweighed in narrow corridors where only one ranking bigwig at a time could get at him. He stored the painful experience in his brain as a reminder. From that day on, boldness and defiance seemed outwardly at least to hide the remains of his old devil *Fear* that had so nearly defeated him earlier. He was bolder now than before the battle of the hollow cottonwood and craftier than most of his kind. During his exile, he had learned plenty of dirty pool and Sunday punches.

There were many examples of foolishness that backfired from overboldness and cocky defiance. On October 6, for instance, Ringo, the bear, and I discovered a generous stand of blueberries (huckleberries) in an isolated location, for some reason overlooked by all local mammals. There is nothing sweeter or tastier than blueberries touched by the magic wand of Jack Frost. My two friends and I stripped the last berry, gorging ourselves in order to keep any neighbors from discovering and sharing the delicious fruit. The three of us moaned and groaned most of the night with bellyaches.

Our stomach upsets quite forgotten in a couple of days, the cold reality of *now* again overtook us. Misty, freezing ground fog and black frost, called "frost smoke," had settled over the Nicomen basin on the night of the seventh. The two bushwhackers were confined to camp because predators lurked in the dense fog, just waiting for either adventurer to try his or her luck. Like a ghostly basketball above the mist, the sun produced at best a watery orange light that lent an unreal tone to the environs while it lasted . . . but what an atmosphere for congeniality on Speculation Log from which I tossed squaw wood and pinecones onto the fire and designed air castles by the hour.

By that late date most seed gatherers and grazers had either moved to lower altitudes or had surrendered to hibernation. Few insects remained that trout could catch; consequently, my fly fishing improved. But the fog that confined one lively bear and one mettlesome raccoon provided favorable climate for devilment sooner or later.

While mature bears may boast some of the sharpest brains in the woodlands, a mature raccoon outsmarts the yearling bruin by a safe margin. Under conditions of forced confinement, Wahnoma spent time at her shrine-tree where at last she fell asleep on her back, paws outstretched. Not a very intelligent position, considering a wide awake Ringo on the Log. He speculated. He may have fancied that I would share in the fun he was about to create during those hours of weather-dictated idleness. Quietly I watched the scoundrel climb the sacred bear-tree. At the most expeditious moment the stinker launched himself into space and made an all-points landing on Noma's belly button. The dirty trick certainly captured the bear's attention, but Ringo scudded out of range into the forest before she could get to her feet.

Buzzing like a bumblebee, Noma walked to the fire pit and haunched, infuriated, not quite sure what she should do to punish that little whelp. With full attention now from his audience, the nervy clown returned to camp and prepared to include Noma and me in his next scheme before she could remember to avenge the last.

Like a miniature gorilla, he strutted back and forth. He had often seen me use the ax that I had pinched from the wolverine to chop firewood, despite its dull, rusty, and totally dangerous condition. Ringo and I had grown so close that our communication signals had matured right along with our friendship. On that misty day, however, I failed to get his message until he had rudely wakened Noma.

119

Then two seemingly unrelated subjects were presented in rapid succession.

First, the raccoon and the bear began clearing a space in front of the tent, Noma's postforage sleeping quarters. Somehow I got the idea that she would like a shelter. So, I picked up the ax, chopped down some young lodgepoles, and built a lean-to in front of the tent. The roof and walls, inside and out, took chinking of sphagnum moss to keep out wind, rain, and frost. Both animals raced around in boundless delight while I padded the finished interior with dry moss, but neither one offered any form of help during the construction.

More and more often Noma foraged at night instead of accompanying Ringo and me in the morning. At first I allowed her to sleep on the tent floor after having removed the sleeping bag, but with the lean-to established as her very own, she never went inside the tent again. Still, it was difficult to keep that slick raccoon from pestering her daytime rest. After several hefty swats, he learned to stay away while she slept in the afternoons.

You may find it hard to believe the second episode that occurred later that afternoon, a startling example of so-called *lower* animal thought. I had no sooner finished the bear's shelter than she took the ax in her mouth and ran into the forest. For a moment it looked as if she planned to return the "borrowed" tool to the wolverine. Ringo yanked at my jeans and churred: his signal to follow. Both animals stopped at the foot of a dead and hollow larch about seventy yards up the hillside from

120

camp. The tree was much too small in diameter for a den even if I knocked myself out to fell it. Again I failed to get the message until Ringo climbed to the first knothole, crammed in his arm up to the shoulder, came out with a fistful of honeycomb, and stared down at me while he licked his fingers.

Because it was too cold for bee activity, it took less than two hours to chop down the tree and split open the trunk. We all feasted on honey until we could hold no more. For a week afterward terrible midnight clashes took place around that shattered trunk as wildlings fought to satisfy a sweet tooth. We saw the wolverine eat dead wood to which honeycomb had once been attached.

Both bear and raccoon preferred fish to honey, so I fished every day. Many of my own "original" menus, however, ended in disappointment—to say the least. I could ruin a freeze-dried camp dinner that required only an addition of boiling water. To conceal my despairing kitchen "talent," huge portions of chili powder, onion flakes, garlic, and spiced salt went into the stewpot. Neither Noma nor Ringo ever refused any of my cookery, proof of unsophisticated appetites.

At about ten o'clock on the "drizzerable" morning of October 10, my eye caught movement where Heather Trail zigzagged into view at timberline. A powerful young Indian with a rucksack slowly left the trail and headed toward our campfire. He was soaked to the skin.

From his rhythmic steps, however, I assumed that his drizzly hike from the Similkameen Valley had been a far less strenuous undertaking for him than it had been for me in dry weather. When he grinned, the soupy cloud cover that formed a lid over our basin seemed to lift. I recognized his once-white Stetson.

11

Clark Tallreed

"GOOD morning!" I said as the man plodded toward the smoky fire pit. I suspected that he might be unfriendly, because I had a bear in "captivity." Okanagan Crees love bears . . . free bears! They are sometimes rough on people who detain their ancestral totemic patron symbol.

"Hi!" he said wearily with a broad smile. He removed his pack. His dripping, wide-brimmed Stetson made him appear taller than six-foot-six. He was about thirty years old, obviously at home in any outdoor situation. He was big enough that a bear would think twice before taking a swing at him. He had tied his long, black braids together while he climbed that backbreaking trail. His jacket, jeans, and boots were squishy wet. Anybody else would have groaned in misery. Crees don't groan.

We shook hands and exchanged names. He was Clark Tallreed. I knew he was the Indian I had seen at Hampton Campground. He studied me with steel-gray eyes that could reduce a man to his lowest common denominator in less than a minute. You couldn't have

hidden a secret from those penetrating eyes. He was a man who would turn away without so much as a whisper and just keep right on going if he didn't like what he saw.

"I'm from Placer Valley country east of here," he said as he warmed his hands at the fire. "I work in the Park between June and October—everything from collecting garbage to settling fights between flatlanders. I heard what that MP said to you. I don't give a hoot what happens to any coon, but Crees and Okanagans hold bears as totemic spirits."

He untied his two dripping braids and settled his gaze on Wahnoma. When he smiled his whole face seemed to warm up—all but those icy eyes that were bred and born to remain like glaciers for his lifetime.

124

"I guessed you're of Salisian extraction," I said. "Okanagan Cree?"

"Yeah. We believe the spirits of dead Indians—decent ones, that is—live on in the bodies of bears. My people from the time of the Ancient One have respected bears. So, I came up here to find out what you intend to do with this yearling."

I strongly suspected that he already knew Noma, that he had sent her away from the public campgrounds because he feared some unthinking clod might do her in for a bear rug. Her behavior also indicated that she and Clark Tallreed weren't exactly strangers. When he nodded a signal she walked from her shelter and haunched against his legs at Speculation Log. Ringo and his guilty conscience had scooted up a lodgepole when the Indian walked into camp. He sat on the highest branch and kept up an uninterrupted chirping. He was probably hinting for someone to invite him to climb down and join the party.

"I don't honestly know what to do with these animals, Clark," I said. "Weather gets worse every day. Grub's low. I won't be able to last until the bear goes into hibernation. That could be as late as December, maybe January. I may take Ringo with me . . . that's the raccoon. You heard the MPs. I'm scared the bear will try to follow me back down the trail. Is there any other way out of the Nicomen wilderness—another trail that doesn't pass that campground? As a Cree, what would you do?"

"In the first place, no Cree would interfere with the

125

will of our Great Spirit. We don't believe human beings are in charge of the woods. Far from it. We don't call native species *wild,* and we never speak of an unspoiled area as *wilderness.* Those are white men's words."

So far he had not answered my questions. I tried to prompt him. "Big predators up here sit and wait for that yearling to get a mile from camp. Right now they are afraid of my rocks and alpenstock. In my opinion it seems your Great Spirit would command *somebody* to look out for this bear until she can take care of herself."

He tossed his head back as if I had shown disrespect for his Great Spirit. So very few whites have understood how to speak honestly with Indians. Clark Tallreed sat as straight as an arrow and X-rayed me with those cold gray eyes.

"There are three trails," he said at last. "As an Indian, I'm not sure yet what I would do. Maybe nothing. I'd like to study what's going on if I may . . . for a few days?"

"Sure. Now how about a cup of coffee to start with? Then we'll stir up something more substantial."

"Good! Thanks!"

The campfire had warmed and relaxed his frame of mind as well as his body. He still dripped from head to foot.

"I'll stack the fire so you can dry out," I said. "We'd be much obliged if you'd camp here with us."

While Clark fried thick cornmeal bannock cakes, I rushed to the lake and caught four large trout. Ringo slipped down from his treetop sanctuary for the fish entrails. Once on the ground, he rushed to me and pretended to hide behind my legs. He clung to my poncho with both hands and peered around at Clark Tallreed like a bashful child. At the come-and-get-it signal, however, he threw all caution to the wind and barged in for his share. In keeping with his true character, the gutty raccoon seized the largest fish from the grill and began to shuck off the skin even though the broiling trout burned his hands. Noma pointed her nose toward the clouds, moaned softly, and waited for me to *hand* her a fish. Ringo never once stopped staring at Clark. He jumped, squawked, and prepared to scoot away every time the man shifted his position on the Log. His trout eaten, the brat dashed for the tent before I could save the sleeping bag from his muddy feet and greasy fingers.

After gulping what was to her a starvation breakfast, Noma continued to haunch against Clark's legs as if she had known him for a full year of her life. He gave her half his trout and a bannock hoecake.

"I've enough grub to stay well into October," Clark said, "but the bear won't go to sleep till the middle of December at the earliest. We gotta do something before then. How come you gave her a Cree name?"

"I don't know. Cousin in Alberta by the name of Friendly Bear. *Wahnoma* was the first tag that crossed my mind."

Clark laughed convulsively when I told him how Ringo and I had met Wahnoma. At length he asked for all the information I could give him about the bear. I handed him my logbook notes. An hour later, after reading from cover to cover, he spoke so softly that I had to sit close to him in order to hear his words.

"Bob, you go on and on about Sasquatch . . . Bigfoot . . . American Yeti . . . in spite of your plaster castings of Wahnoma's prints. Are you willing to listen to another story about Sasquatch? I heard my father tell it many years ago."

"Okay," I said, feeling a bit sheepish after he had read every secret comment in my entire notebook. "I've just about written off the whole myth."

Obviously Clark Tallreed did not believe in Sasquatch.

"This yarn is only some sixty years old," he said. "It started when a Hollywood outfit came up to this country to film scenes for a Gargantua-type horror movie called *Ingagi*. One evening after a day's filming, some of the wags in the company dressed up in ape costumes and played monkey in a little village by the name of Osoyoos. Scared the whey out of local farmers who never learned the truth. The same creeps pulled the same caper over in Washington. Same results.

"I hope your plaster castings make sense in L.A. There are people up here, though, who would still believe in Sasquatch even if you undressed one of those Hollywood 'extras' right in front of them. Every year some hunter gets three sheets to the wind, sees a bear walking around on his hind paws, and swears on the Bible he's seen Bigfoot. Qualified biologists have argued that no Sasquatch could possibly exist *anywhere* in the world today—much less in the Pacific Northwest."

After finishing his pipe and coffee, Clark set up his

128

tent and began to organize his gear. He ignored wet clothing and the possibility of more rain. Having eyed every move the Indian made, Ringo slipped from my tent. He climbed the Log for a better view. While pretending to be the picture of idleness, he took mental snapshots of each shiny object in Clark's equipment. I warned the Indian who thought Ringo was just being droll.

Without moving his head, the raccoon sat next to me and ogled with pop-eyed curiosity. It dawned on me that he may have sensed that my time to leave had arrived and that Clark—who "didn't give a hoot what happened to coons"—was about to take over. It might have been possible that Ringo entertained a thought of having to live alone again: starvation, poor shelter, slow legs on which to outrun swarms of fast predators. On that same morning daggers of ice around the edge of the lake predicated the arrival of winter before long. Clark carried a thermometer which to my surprise read 32° F. The unhappy raccoon must have known that his deep-water defense against his enemies would disappear once the lake froze over.

I saw what I interpreted as continuing mystery in Ringo's expression when he stared into my eyes on October 12. His wounds had almost healed, but his attitude had not improved. Skipping no details, I told Clark of our experiences with the raccoon colony and asked his advice. The Okanagan Cree examined his own careful conclusions.

"You might try again," he said after a long stare at the lake, "but if you leave him there without full acceptance by the other coons, I'll bet you ten bucks they'll gut him the minute you're outta sight."

Clark understood the ways of native animals better than most people, certainly better than I did. He proved it in the way Noma took to him, in the way he dismissed cock-and-bull yarns about Sasquatch, and in sensitive perception of all life in the northwoods. I insisted upon one last effort to reunite Ringo with his kin before deciding to take him home with me.

Summer clothing only partially shielded me against the gloomy journey to those frost-bound cottonwoods, while Ringo's natural winter coat did its intended job. He ignored the cold. Mindful of blinkless eyes that stared from tangles of icicled underbrush on both sides of the narrow canyon, we devoted every moment to alertness as we picked a frosty way alongside the barely trickling creek. We shared the same nervous anxieties. I caught myself repeating his signals when he whispered, snapped his eyelids, twitched his lips, snorted, side-stepped, clacked his fingernails, and gurgled his belly by swallowing air into his stomach. Sharp little cackly burps meant stop on the spot to verify suspicious movements. About the only thing impossible for me to do was crawl in flattened positions with a tail that dragged! He may have believed in good-luck charms, for he carried from time to time small sticks, stones, leaves, or feathers. Could that tendency have been learned from the polished adamant he knew I always carried in my right

130

pocket—the one my grandfather wore for luck throughout the Civil War? Ringo had not just burdened himself with extra weight under those precarious circumstances; what he carried must have expressed a belief in *something*. I had a good deal less faith in the adamant.

The raccoon jogged along, most of the way over squeaky ice crystals, as if eager to make the trip, which led me further to suppose that he sensed my intention to leave soon. He may have faced the urgency of winter quarters. Nicomen Creek Canyon was a shaded deep-freeze even at its confluence with the Skaist—a dark, silent, inhospitable gorge.

Across the river from Raccoonville, we gasped at the display of belligerence. Shrieking ominously and pounding the icy mud with their "hands," *twelve* ugly-tempered demonstrators picketed the right bank of the Skaist and dared us to cross. The noisy coons had appeared so unexpectedly in the dormant canyon that shock-value alone was enough to turn us back. The "dirty dozen" smelled blood. They craved revenge for our last visit. Neither Ringo nor I boasted the grit to oppose such a force.

Our question answered, we wasted no time heading back up the frozen canyon. In a clearing near the outlet of Nicomen Lake, Mrs. Mephitis and her five Xerox copies were digging ant eggs from a rotten log. Ringo joined the family like a welcome kissing cousin. I feared our unpolluted air might soon come to an end; but the rogue of Nicomen Lake got along with those strange

131

associates, and somehow he communicated the message that the two-legger could be considered a friend also . . . but not that clumsy bear! I was delighted that Noma was with Clark Tallreed. At first the five Xeroxes distrusted the raccoon's overfamiliar fingers. He simply *had* to explore each kit. With all preliminaries accomplished, my hands, feet, and legs received a thorough sniffing with no threat of heavy artillery.

At length the little skunks pawed and pinched the raccoon, bit him, clawed him, and climbed on top of him for an old-fashioned "hog-pile." Mrs. Mephitis ordinarily allowed no male animal, including Papa Mephitis, to go near her little stinkers. So, I had to conclude that Ringo was a special favorite of the mother. In any event, the scalawag found out what it was like to absorb the poking and teasing he had dished out so generously to Noma and me, except that he had the advantage of a thick outer coat as well as dense woolen underwear for protection— an edge the skinny bear and I lacked.

As the cleverest North American animal with his "hands," he carefully maneuvered Mrs. Mephitis's black-and-white quintuplets with the soft kid gloves for which his species is famous. Once free from the five wrestlers, he climbed swiftly to my shoulders and whispered what I hoped was, "Let's split!" If there was one thing I did not need it was five fully armed skunklets climbing to my shoulders in pursuit of Ringo.

12

The Earth Mother's Way

JOGGING back along the lakeshore, Ringo uttered windy sighs that I interpreted as his expression of a blue mood. Only with trotting stride could a man keep up with the bounder when he longed to rejoin Noma. He could run a little faster if he was frightened or irritated, but without pressures, he was lamentably slow for his own good. Cold had numbed my feet and legs to the extent that running was painfully uncoordinated. When I stumbled and fell, Ringo stopped and waited for me to get on my feet.

Running to meet us, Clark and Noma paced rapidly down the beach.

"They refused to accept him." Clark took it for granted. Otherwise, I would have returned alone.

When I recovered my breath, I told him that twelve colonists had dared us to cross the Skaist. "I'll have to take him to the city with me."

"Bob, that would be foul ball in the eyes of an Okanagan Cree," Clark said. A deep frown creased his forehead as he shook his head and ripped me to shreds with knify gray eyes. "Crated in a box in the belly of a DC-10! Scared to death! Ringo is a *forest-marsh* animal. No city dweller. In L.A. he'd be like a frog in the Queen's punch bowl. He'd starve himself, hankering for his native Cascades. I'm not sure yet what the answer is. But your solution is *not* the Earth Mother's way."

Later that same afternoon Noma and Ringo rolled in the wet sand and sassed one another while Clark and I fished and debated our problems. A trout-and-tuber diet had filled Noma's muscles with excess energy. As she sat later on a boulder studying her image in the lake and goofing off, she slapped lightly at her reflection in the water—lightly to be on the safe side in the event that "other bear" decided to swat back.

"Our trout have all but quit biting, Bob," Clark said when we returned to camp with fewer fish than usual. "When you see those thin, blue spaces between clouds, and the wind sounds like ripping canvas, you can bet your bottom dollar on snow." The signs were there.

We removed our gloves to thaw out our hands over a gurgling volcano of somersaulting red beans. Noma left Ringo in order to sit with Clark by the fire. It was touching to see a wild animal and a human being so devoted one to the other. Clark Tallreed himself was naturally unusual. He finally admitted that he had cared for the bear when she left her family group much younger than a yearling. So, he confirmed at last that they weren't strangers, although he said he had done nothing to tame or domesticate her.

134

The Indian and Noma now spent most daylight hours at forage. They climbed above the berms of buckwheat and heather to the open meadows east of the lake where the bear upturned slabs of flagstone for grubs and larvae—and an occasional vole. When her belly had partially filled out, they left the open hillsides in order to explore the vast dense canyon forest below Nicomen Ridge. In thick marsh reeds or deep in the gorge of the Skaist River headwaters, the Okanagan Cree taught the bear an easy way to catch frogs, a method known only to backwoods Indians and mother bears. At night he shared his food, his place on the Log, and his tent with the bear. They were rarely apart.

After October 15 Ringo resumed some of his natural habit of wandering alone in order to forage what he could still find on the buckwheat meadows. Clark assured me that large predators no longer climbed to the wintry uplands, and that Ringo knew that his last dangerous enemy had gone down the trail to "easier pickings." Late each afternoon Clark would challenge us to a quick "stand-up" bath in the icy lake. He alone enjoyed that spectacle of Indian toughness, but the two animals and I tortured ourselves with quick dips rather than have him think we were chicken!

On the night of October 21 the "Old Man of the North" slunk in while we slept. He dropped a ghostly overlay of snow that changed our autumn world into the white crystalline kingdom of winter. A northwesterly soon cleared the sky as it does after the first snow, but air temperatures dropped and stayed below freezing. My hopeless struggle to hold back the clock had reached its only possible conclusion. My thin-skinned tent that allowed freezing drafts and moisture to penetrate—as well as Clark's ridiculous "stand-up" baths—sent me almost to the verge of defeat.

Ringo and I ran to the lake on the morning of the twenty-second. The water had iced out about six feet beyond the shoreline. If that Indian thought he'd get either the raccoon or me in that lake again. . . .

Without a word after breakfast, Clark took down his tent and packed his rucksack. We all knew the hour had come.

"My friend," he said when he had shouldered his pack, "I'll leave you grub for a week. Wahnoma and I will head up Pinto Creek, then over Three Brothers Pass—up yonder where the Creator piled all those mountains against the sky. Over a shortcut to my valley. Placer Creek country. The coon couldn't keep up." He was too polite to say that I couldn't either. "I'll hibernate the bear this winter in my cabin and turn her out come Moon-of-the-Moose-Child (June). That's our Earth Mother's way. You stick around this basin for a week maybe. See what happens, huh? Come back some day, you hear?"

My eyes watered up and a lump in my throat kept me from saying anything. He read my expression. Then he smiled as if he guarded a secret I didn't know. When we removed our gloves and shook hands, Noma stood and

136

whined. I hugged her great head and shoulders. Before
following Clark, she ran to her tree, embraced it,
chewed the bark, and left the scent of her urine. When
the Indian whistled, she rushed to Ringo, licked him
across the face, swatted him gently, and finally raced
toward the beach to catch up with her adored Cree man-
of-learning.

From a rise at the edge of the forest, Ringo and I sat
on a snow-covered boulder and watched as the two dark
forms of our friends grew smaller along the sparkling
shoreline. Suddenly the raccoon bolted away after them.
Five minutes later Clark and the bear stopped and
waited for the screaming Ringo to catch up. Through
binoculars I saw the Indian remove his pack and sit down
on the snow. He also took off his gloves. Noma haunched
beside him. When Ringo reached them, Clark took the
raccoon on his knee. From a cloud of breath vapor I
assumed he was giving the word to that naughty little

scamp. Slowly he set the rascal down, stood up, shouldered his pack, and motioned for the bear to follow.

Clark Tallreed: true son of the northland in the grandest manner of our Earth Mother's guiding principles.

Ringo sat alone until his freezing fanny reminded him of the campfire. So, he got to his feet and crept slowly back to camp, dragging his fluffy, black-ringed tail in the snow. Invariably you could determine his state of mind by the position of that tail.

For three days the weather remained fair. Ringo and I scrounged for grubs in every forest clearing not under snow. Hardening frost of an evening rang with metallic droplets of sound that seemed to intensify the frigid silence of twilight. Orange plumes from squaw wood embers cast shadows among the snow-draped lodgepoles behind us, where not one predator now lingered in the frozen forest, including that diehard wolverine. Each night Ringo and I sat on Speculation Log, hovering over the fire pit until after the first *dance macabre* of crackling northern lights, the aurora borealis.

On the twenty-fifth a skimpy two-day ration remained in the rucksack. No fish could be coaxed to rise through broken holes in the icy for fly, spinner, or bait. It appeared that all life had slipped from the basin. On the night of the twenty-seventh when we shared our last food, I promised Ringo we would hit the trail next morning at sunup. He crammed his "hands"—about as warm as icicles—between my shirt and the back of my neck.

138

The shock made me yell. In his own way I am sure he laughed, because he kept his hands there until they were warm.

On the twenty-eighth I was folding the tent shortly after sunrise when Ringo began to churr like a hoarse ptarmigan. He tugged at my jeans without taking his eyes from the lakeshore.

"Sorry, old man, we can't hack it here any longer. We don't have one bite of grub for breakfast. Come on! Let's hike out and find some chow!"

He yo-yoed in front of me, tugging me toward the clearing above the beach.

Two dark bodies barely within sight crunched over the frozen snow along the shoreline, but because breath vapor preceded them, they were impossible to identify. I focused the binoculars, but warmth from my eyebrows caused the exit pupils to fog over and I could not see through them. At length two large boar raccoons headed toward camp as fast as they could maneuver the slick crust on the snow. Uneasy and puzzled, Ringo beat the snow with one hand and my knee with the other.

A single notion struck me: The colony had sent two husky hit-men to kill Ringo, so he would make no further attempts to winter in Raccoonville. I ran for the alpenstock and posed like Rod Carew at the bat. I had lavished too much on that rogue to allow any animal to do him in. How I wished Noma and Clark were there!

When the two husky bruisers arrived and swaggered into camp, it was obvious that each one was almost twice

139

Ringo's size. My *protégé* hackled his guard hair like a potbellied porcupine. He ignored my command to get his butt on my shoulders. With a chilling battle cry, he charged the first male in order to win the advantages an attacker always has. The big boar crouched, covered his face, and whined. He refused to fight! I had never before seen a raccoon turn down a good brawl.

With jaws chomping like Spanish castanets, Ringo flung himself at the second *macho* and set his long, sharp teeth around the stranger's windpipe. The bruiser rolled over in the snow and exposed his belly, the sign of surrender. Ringo—a gentleman that he could be on rare occasions—let go his strategic hold. The three males haunched near the Log and stared in puzzling silence from one to the other, ignoring the fact that I stood ready for my own private war in case the two pulled a secret trick. There was a short *coonfab* among the three. After a two-minute study of faces, Ringo ran to me and tugged my jeans.

For a few shocking moments it looked as if I had *three* outcast ruffians on my hands to make an already difficult problem impossible. I could guess the expression on that gold-braided MP's face when I walked in with three raccoons. A zoo near Vancouver might take two of them, a grim solution—one that Clark Tallreed would never forgive.

But Ringo and I had perfected our communication signals to the extent that I knew he was urging me to follow him. I looked up at the high cirrus clouds corrugating the sky, an absolutely unmistakable sign of approaching heavy weather. Being a raccoon, Ringo suspected trickery from *any* two of his kind. He demanded me as his back-up man in the event of a hoax.

Fearing hypothermia, I put on all my extra garments before leaving.

Along the icy beach I ran behind the three boars that suddenly expressed an insane hurry toward Nicomen Creek Canyon. Their coats covered with rime from breath vapor and kicked-up snow, the trio raced along the path the two emissaries had broken in the frosty crust. I all but flipped at a horrible mental picture: Supposing those tricky fiends were leading my friend to his execution in Raccoonville! Ringo may have suspected the same thing.

They picked a thornless route over snowdrifts down the frozen canyon, arriving within an hour at the Skaist River cottonwood grove. I counted fourteen masked faces staring at us in silence from the riverbank and from naked trees as the three males skidded across the frozen stream.

Shifting from one cold foot to the other on the left bank, I still wondered why Ringo had insisted that I accompany him and the two husky strangers to Raccoonville. In the habit of studying his victims before a theft, he probably suspected trouble simply as a habitual way of thinking. In such an event, he would need me to swing the alpenstock as he remembered I had swung on

141

fishers, coyotes, and the wolverine. When he reached the colony on the right bank, he slowly tested certain members with a light swat to the head and a rear-end sniff.

All fear and doubt simply vanished. Winter quarters now seemed secure.

Let's say he missed the greetings of a fickle mate, but a chorus of churrs from the entire colony made it clear that he had served his exile for whatever offenses he had committed. The group seemed to welcome him warmly to the hollow of the giant cottonwood where the fight had erupted earlier. He turned briefly and flashed a knowing look toward me before entering the den. One ricocheting side glance said it all.

Although no one will ever know what behavior had brought about his expulsion, we are tempted to believe that raccoons don't permanently abandon wicked kinfolk. By the same potato-patch logic, in the Earth Mother's grand design, Ringo was no less a true son of the wilderness than Clark Tallreed or Wahnoma. Just different.

Thus, his problem—and his secret project—achieved solution in nature's own way as predicted by the Okanagan Cree, whose knowing smile I recalled. In my prejudiced opinion Ringo was still a shameless, but nonetheless lovable, scalawag, now a rejoicing scalawag, no doubt planning next spring's mischief. I rejoiced in the hope that he would never again have to follow a human being up that dark and dangerous canyon while

142

serving out a judgment on the flinty shores of Nicomen Lake.

When I arrived in Los Angeles on November 3, ridiculous difficulties beset my efforts to convince my employers that my plaster castings had *not* come from the footprints of an ape-man. Many people had either seen or had personally cast similar molds without realizing the "footprints" were in fact double bearpaw marks. One outraged group of Sasquatch fans hoped I would be prosecuted for giving false security to unarmed backpackers in Bigfoot country.

Although I returned home with no genuine Sasquatch information, I brought back a priceless serendipity instead: unforgettable memories of three lovable companions.